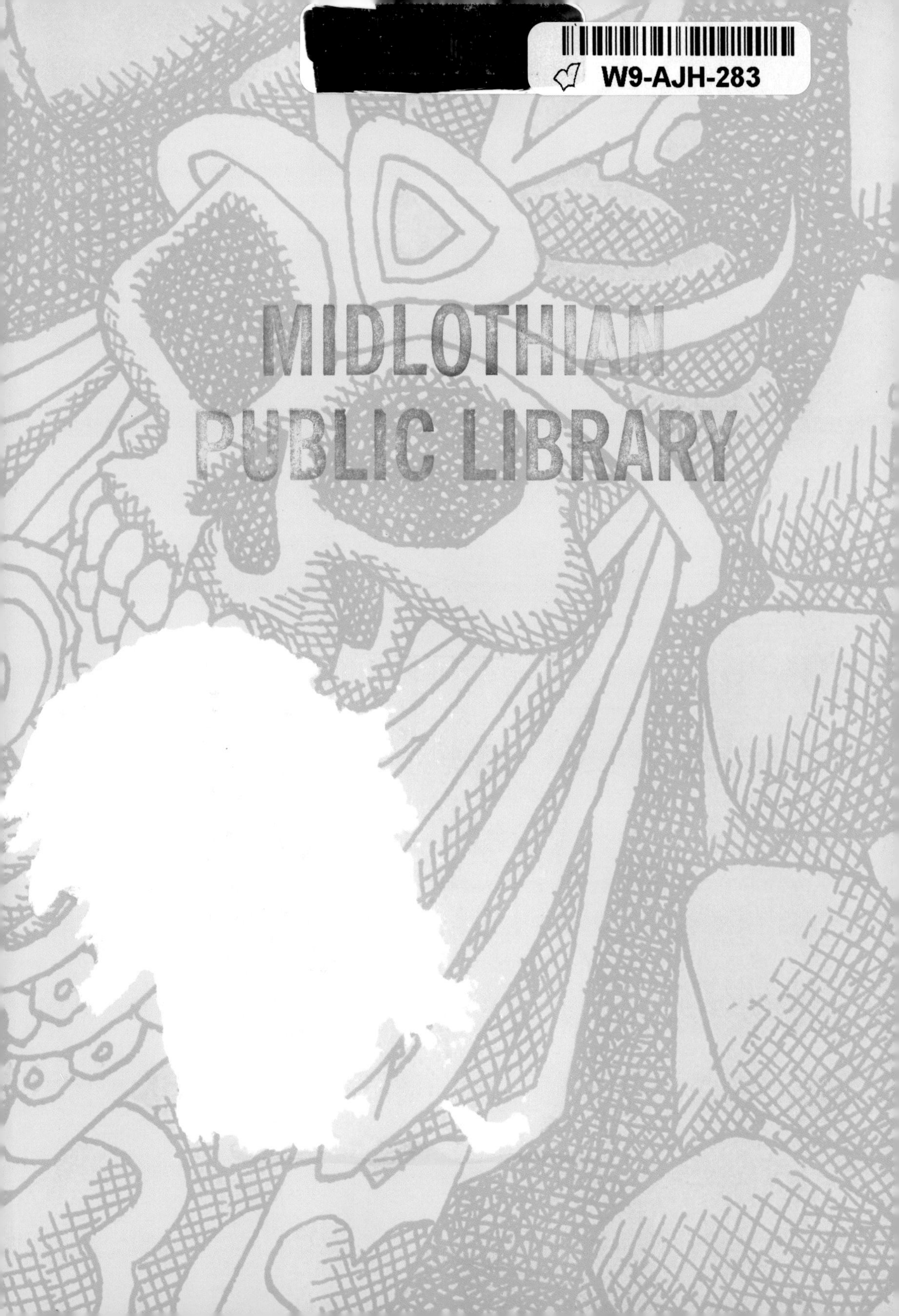

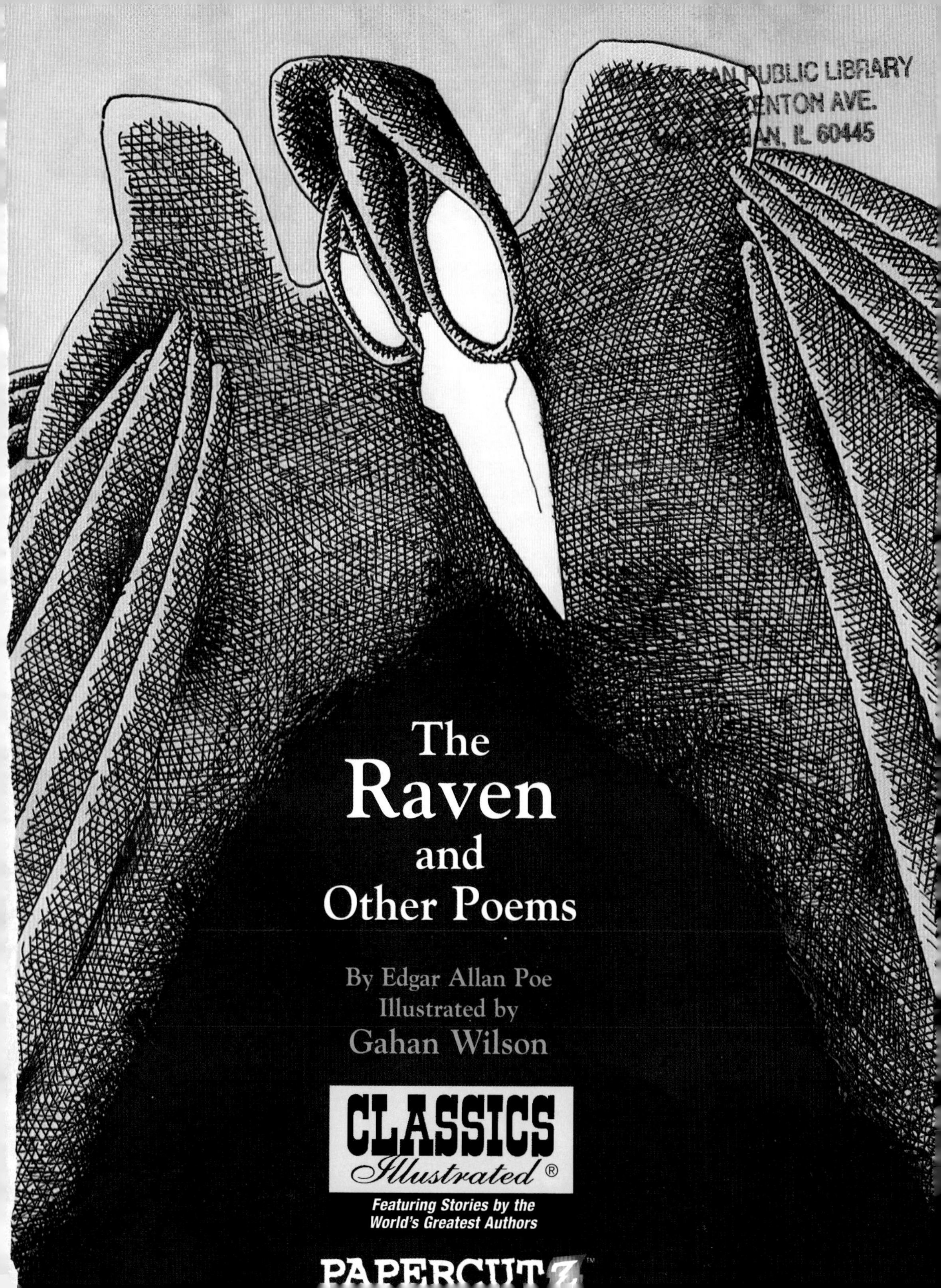

The Raven and Other Poems

By Edgar Allan Poe
Illustrated by
Gahan Wilson

CLASSICS Illustrated®

Featuring Stories by the World's Greatest Authors

PAPERCUTZ™

CLASSICS ILLUSTRATED GRAPHIC NOVELS AVAILABLE FROM PAPERCUTZ

CLASSICS ILLUSTRATED DELUXE:

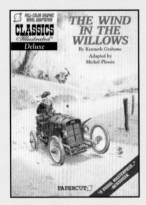

Graphic Novel #1
"The Wind In
The Willows"

Graphic Novel #2
"Tales From The
Brothers Grimm"

Graphic Novel #3
"Frankenstein"

CLASSICS ILLUSTRATED:

Graphic Novel #1
"Great Expectations"

Graphic Novel #2
"The Invisible Man"

Graphic Novel #3
"Through the Looking-Glass"

Featuring Stories by the World's Greatest Authors

#4

The Raven and Other Poems

By Edgar Allan Poe
Illustrated by Gahan Wilson

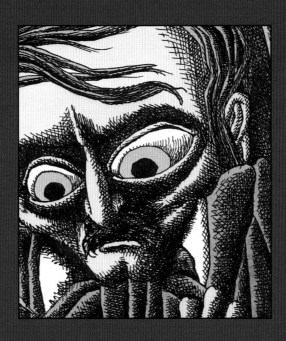

PAPERCUTZ
New York

Masterpieces of the macabre, these elegant poems – drawn from the most fertile period in Edgar Allan Poe's life – delve the dark depths of the subconscious and trace hidden horrors of the human soul. Never before and rarely since has a writer captured so completely the melancholy, the torment, the passion, the grotesque humor and the suspense that is inherent in the battle between human good and evil, between the rational and the irrational. With his contemporary, Nathaniel Hawthorne, Poe was a founder of the American Gothic movement that blossomed before the Civil War. Poe used his own tortured life as an inspiration for his writing, the first volumes of which appeared in 1831. In 1844, following bouts with poverty, alcoholism, and romantic and professional failures, he produced the eerie poem **The Raven** for the New York *Evening News*. The popularity of that poem briefly propelled Poe into the literary spotlight. For the most part, though, he was criticized, demeaned, and condemned as a lunatic and a literary fake: "the jingle man," Ralph Waldo Emerson huffed, dismissing Poe's works as all style and little substance. Only after his death was Poe recognized for his consistent command of mood, emotion, and atmosphere; he was, judged William Yeates, "always and for all lands a great lyric poet." Not only are these fascinating poems among the world's best-loved and most widely read, but they have influenced several generations of writers. Haunting, beautiful, full of rhythm and melody, Poe's forms, techniques, and theories inspired the post-Civil War American Bohemian writers, the French Symbolists, and were also later echoed in the works of such writers as T.S. Eliot and William Faulkner.

The Raven and Other Poems
By Edgar Allan Poe
Illustrated by Gahan Wilson
Wade Roberts, Original Editorial Director
Alex Wald, Original Art Director
Production by Ortho
Classics Illustrated Historian – John Haufe
Editorial Assistant — Michael Petranek
Jim Salicrup
Editor-in-Chief

ISBN 13: 978-1-59707-140-6
ISBN 10: 1-59707-140-4

Printed in China.
Distributed by Macmillan.
10 9 8 7 6 5 4 3 2 1

Table of Contents

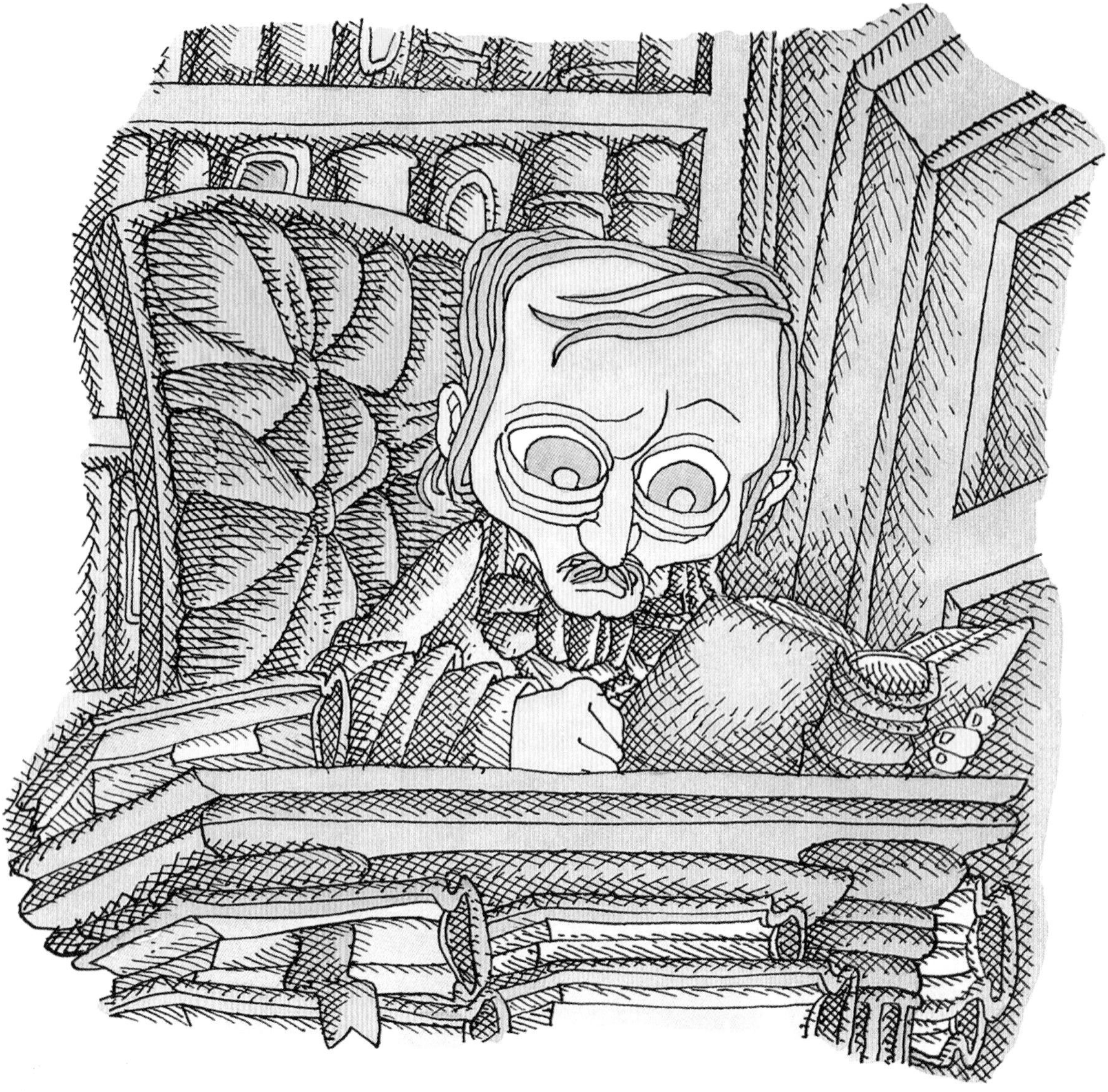

THE RAVEN

Once upon a midnight dreary, while I pondered, weak and weary,
Over many a quaint and curious volume of forgotten lore—
While I nodded, nearly napping, suddenly there came a tapping,
As of some one gently rapping, rapping at my chamber door.
"'Tis some visitor," I muttered, "tapping at my chamber door—
Only this and nothing more."

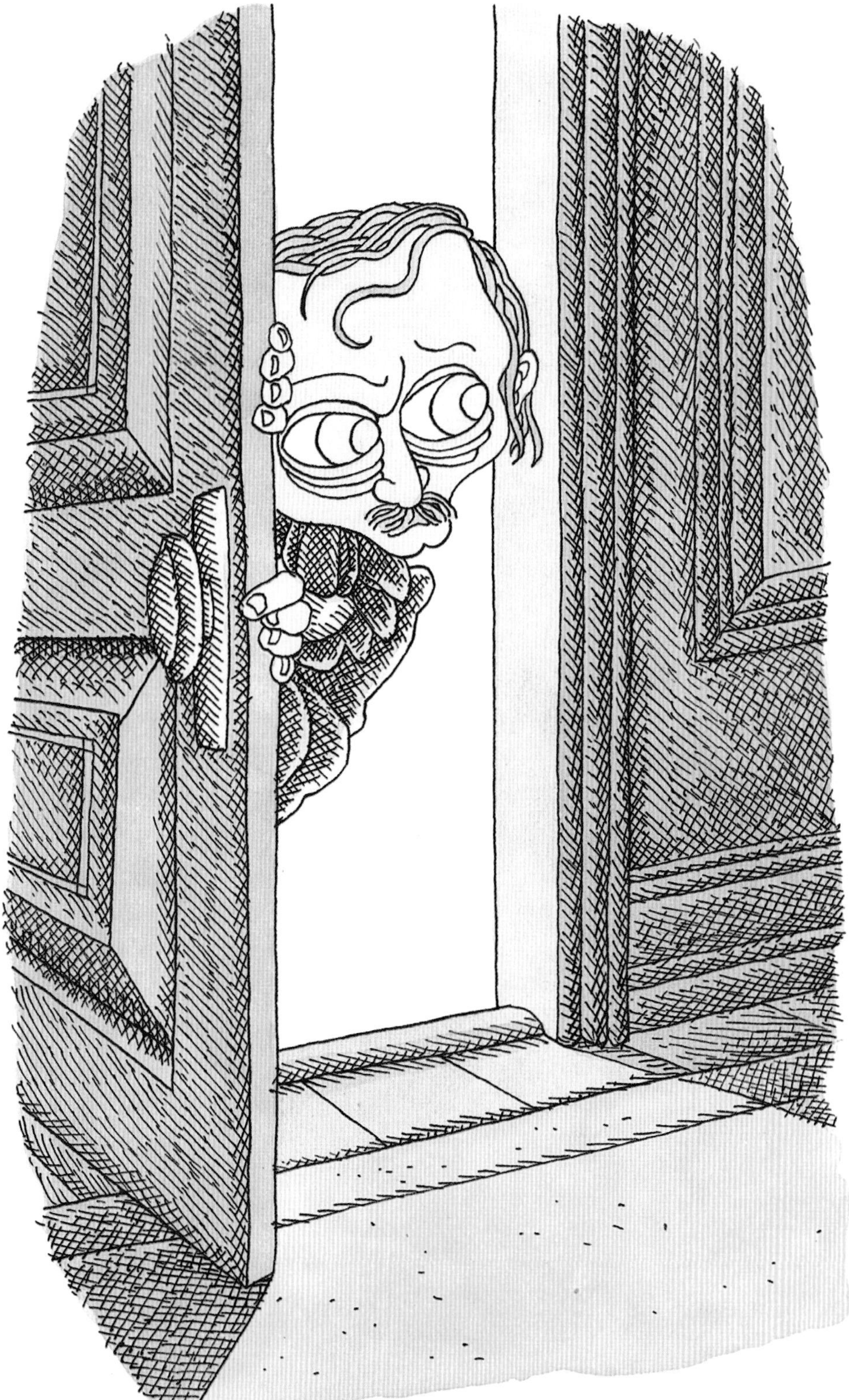

Ah, distinctly I remember, it was in the bleak December,

And each separate dying ember wrought its ghost upon the floor.

Eagerly I wished the morrow;— vainly I had sought to borrow

From my books surcease of sorrow— sorrow for the lost Lenore—

For the rare and radiant maiden whom the angels named Lenore—

Nameless here for evermore.

And the silken sad uncertain rustling of each purple curtain

Thrilled me— filled me with fantastic terrors never felt before;

So that now, to still the beating of my heart, I stood repeating:

"'Tis some visitor entreating entrance at my chamber door—

Some late visitor entreating entrance at my chamber door;

This it is and nothing more."

Presently my soul grew stronger; hesitating then no longer,

"Sir," said I, "or Madam, truly your forgiveness I implore;

But the fact is I was napping, and so gently you came rapping,

And so faintly you came tapping, tapping at my chamber door,

That I scarce was sure I heard you"— here I opened wide the door;—

Darkness there and nothing more.

Deep into that darkness peering, long I stood there wondering, fearing,

Doubting, dreaming dreams no mortals ever dared to dream before;

But the silence was unbroken, and the stillness gave no token,

And the only word there spoken was the whispered word, "Lenore!"

This I whispered, and an echo murmured back the word, "Lenore!"—

Merely this and nothing more.

Back into the chamber turning, all my soul within me burning,
Soon again I heard a tapping something louder than before.
"Surely," said I, "surely that is something at my window lattice;
Let me see, then, what thereat is, and this mystery explore—
Let my heart be still a moment, and this mystery explore;—
'Tis the wind and nothing more."

Open here I flung the shutter, when, with many a flirt and flutter,
In there stepped a stately Raven of the saintly days of yore.
Not the least obeisance made he; not a minute stopped or stayed he,
But, with mien of lord or lady, perched above my chamber door—
Perched upon a bust of Pallas just above my chamber door—
Perched, and sat, and nothing more.

Then this ebony bird beguiling my sad fancy into smiling,
By the grave and stern decorum of the countenance it wore,
"Though thy crest be shorn and shaven, thou," I said, "art sure no craven,
Ghastly grim and ancient Raven wandering from the Nightly shore—
Tell me what thy lordly name is on the Night's Plutonian shore!"
                              Quoth the Raven, "Nevermore."

Much I marvelled this ungainly fowl to hear discourse so plainly,
Though its answer little meaning— little relevancy bore;
For we cannot help agreeing that no living human being
Ever yet was blessed with seeing bird above his chamber door—
Bird or beast upon the sculptured bust above his chamber door,
                              With such name as "Nevermore."

But the Raven, sitting lonely on that placid bust, spoke only
That one word, as if his soul in that one word he did outpour.
Nothing farther then he uttered; not a feather then he fluttered—
Till I scarcely more than muttered: "Other friends have flown before—
On the morrow *he* will leave me as my Hopes have flown before."
                              Then the bird said, "Nevermore."

Startled at the stillness broken by reply so aptly spoken,
"Doubtless," said I, "what it utters is its only stock and store,
Caught from some unhappy master whom unmerciful Disaster
Followed fast and followed faster till his songs one burden bore—
Till the dirges of his Hope that melancholy burden bore
                              Of 'Never— nevermore.'"

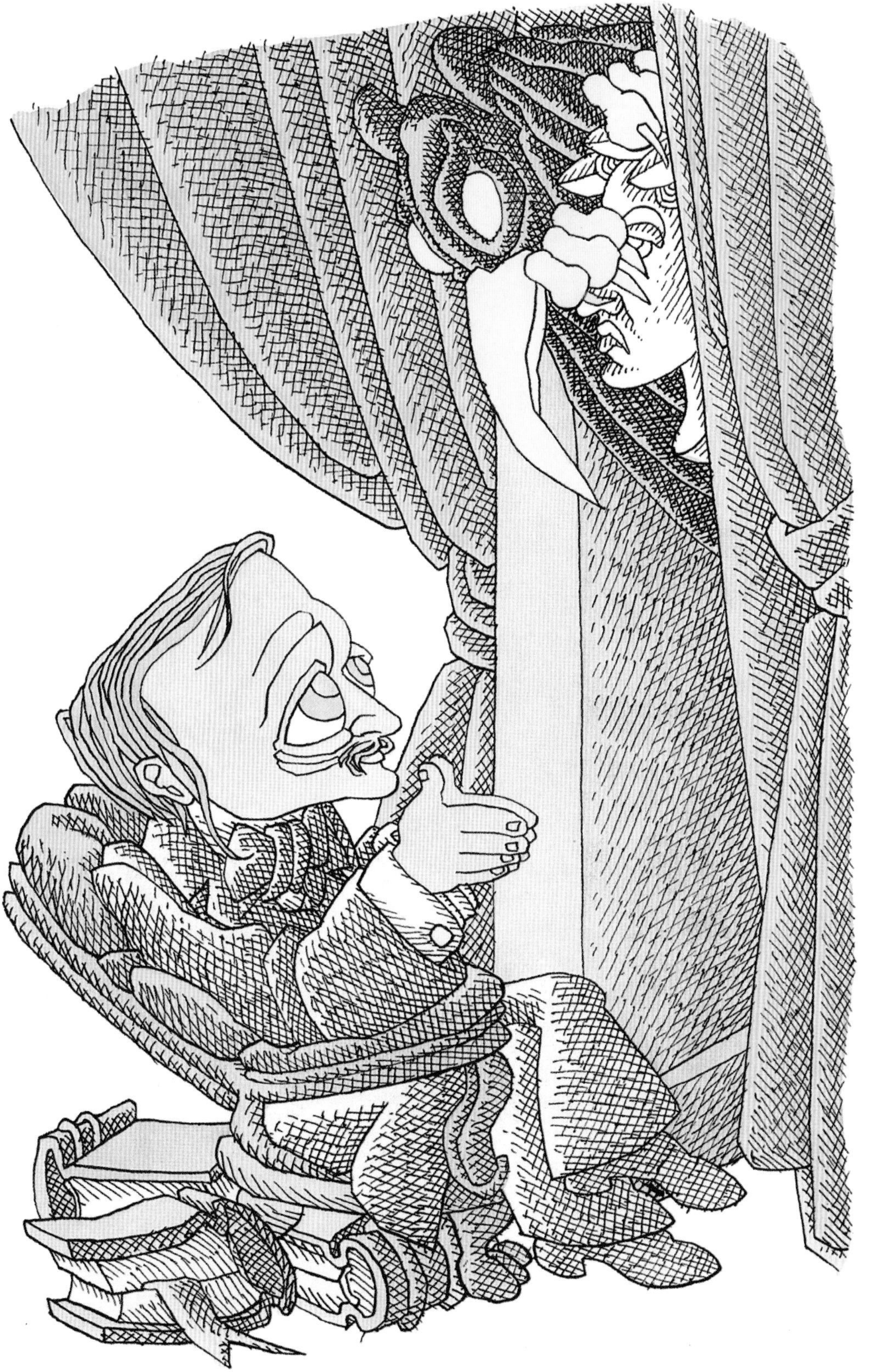

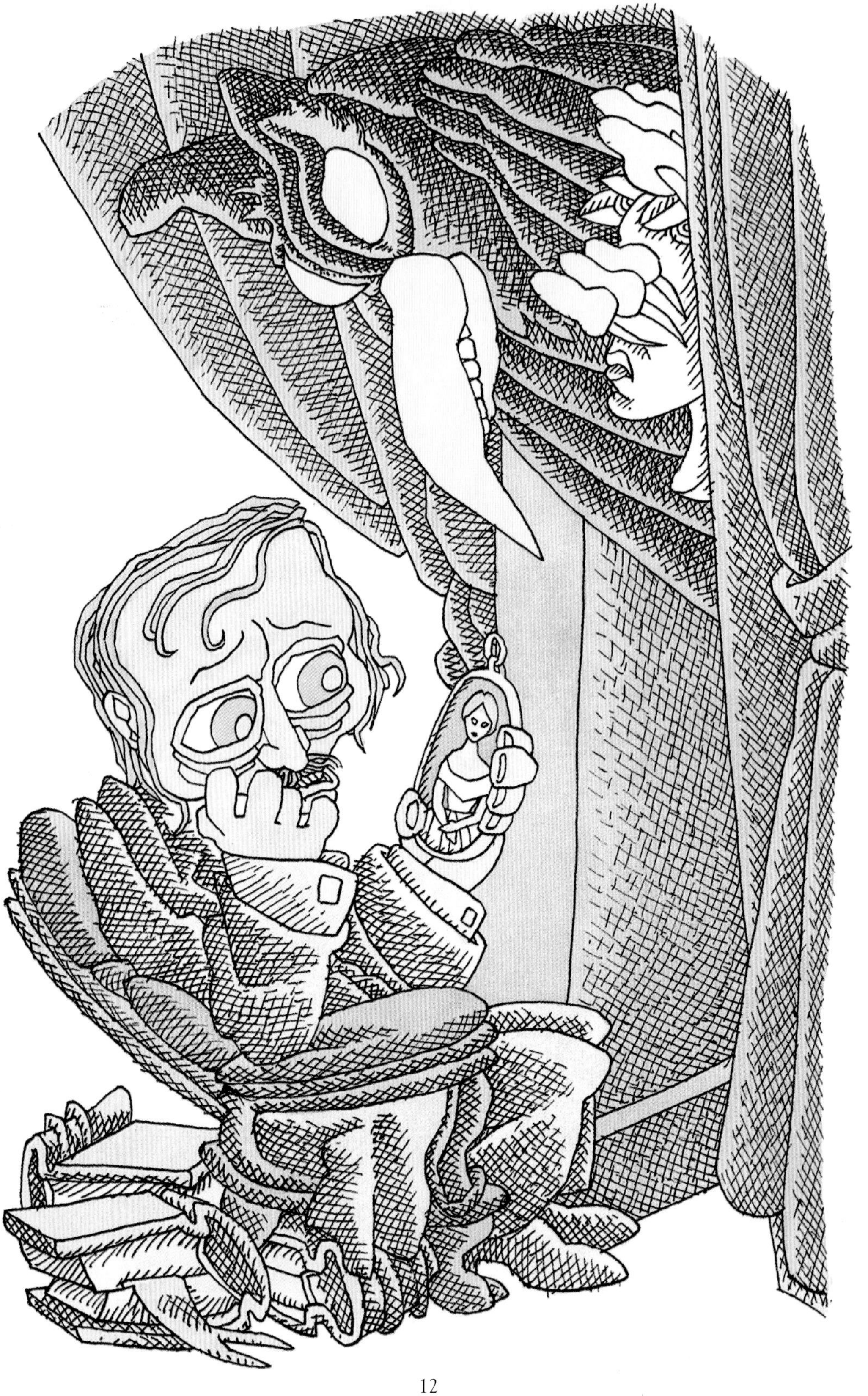

But the Raven still beguiling all my sad soul into smiling,
Straight I wheeled a cushioned seat in front of bird and bust and door;
Then, upon the velvet sinking, I betook myself to linking
Fancy unto fancy, thinking what this ominous bird of yore—
What this grim, ungainly, ghastly, gaunt, and ominous bird of yore
                                        Meant in croaking "Nevermore."

This I sat engaged in guessing, but no syllable expressing
To the fowl whose fiery eyes now burned into my bosom's core;
This and more I sat divining, with my head at ease reclining
On the cushion's velvet lining that the lamp-light gloated o'er,
But whose velvet violet lining with the lamp-light gloating o'er
                                        She shall press, ah, nevermore!

Then, methought, the air grew denser, perfumed from an unseen censer
Swung by Seraphim whose foot-falls tinkled on the tufted floor.
"Wretch," I cried, "thy God hath lent thee— by these angels he hath sent thee
Respite— respite and nepenthe from thy memories of Lenore!
Quaff, oh quaff this kind nepenthe and forget this lost Lenore!"
                                        Quoth the Raven, "Nevermore."

"Prophet!" said I, "thing of evil!— prophet still, if bird or devil!—
Whether Tempter sent, or whether tempest tossed thee here ashore,
Desolate, yet all undaunted, on this desert land enchanted—
On this home by Horror haunted,— tell me truly, I implore—
Is there— *is* there balm in Gilead?— tell me— tell me, I implore!"
                                        Quoth the Raven, "Nevermore."

"Prophet!" said I, "thing of evil!— prophet still, if bird or devil!
By that heaven that bends above us— by that God we both adore—
Tell this soul with sorrow laden if, within the distant Aidenn,
It shall clasp a sainted maiden whom the angels name Lenore—
Clasp a rare and radiant maiden whom the angels name Lenore."
                    Quoth the Raven, "Nevermore."

"Be that word our sign of parting, bird or fiend!" I shrieked, upstarting—
"Get thee back into the tempest and the Night's Plutonian shore!
Leave no black plume as a token of that lie thy soul hath spoken!
Leave my loneliness unbroken!— quit the bust above my door!
Take thy beak from out my heart, and take thy form from off my door!"
                    Quoth the Raven, "Nevermore."

And the Raven, never flitting, still is sitting, still is sitting
On the pallid bust of Pallas just above my chamber door;
And his eyes have all the seeming of a demon's that is dreaming,
And the lamp-light o'er him streaming throws his shadow on the floor;
And my soul from out that shadow that lies floating on the floor
                    Shall be lifted— nevermore!

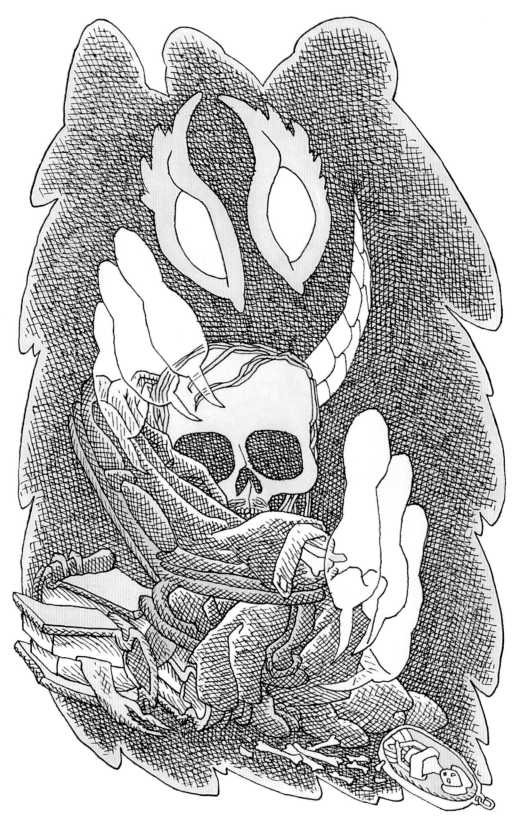

ANNABEL LEE

It was many and many a year ago,
In a kingdom by the sea,
That a maiden there lived whom you may know
By the name of Annabel Lee
And this maiden she lived with no other thought
Than to love and be loved by me.

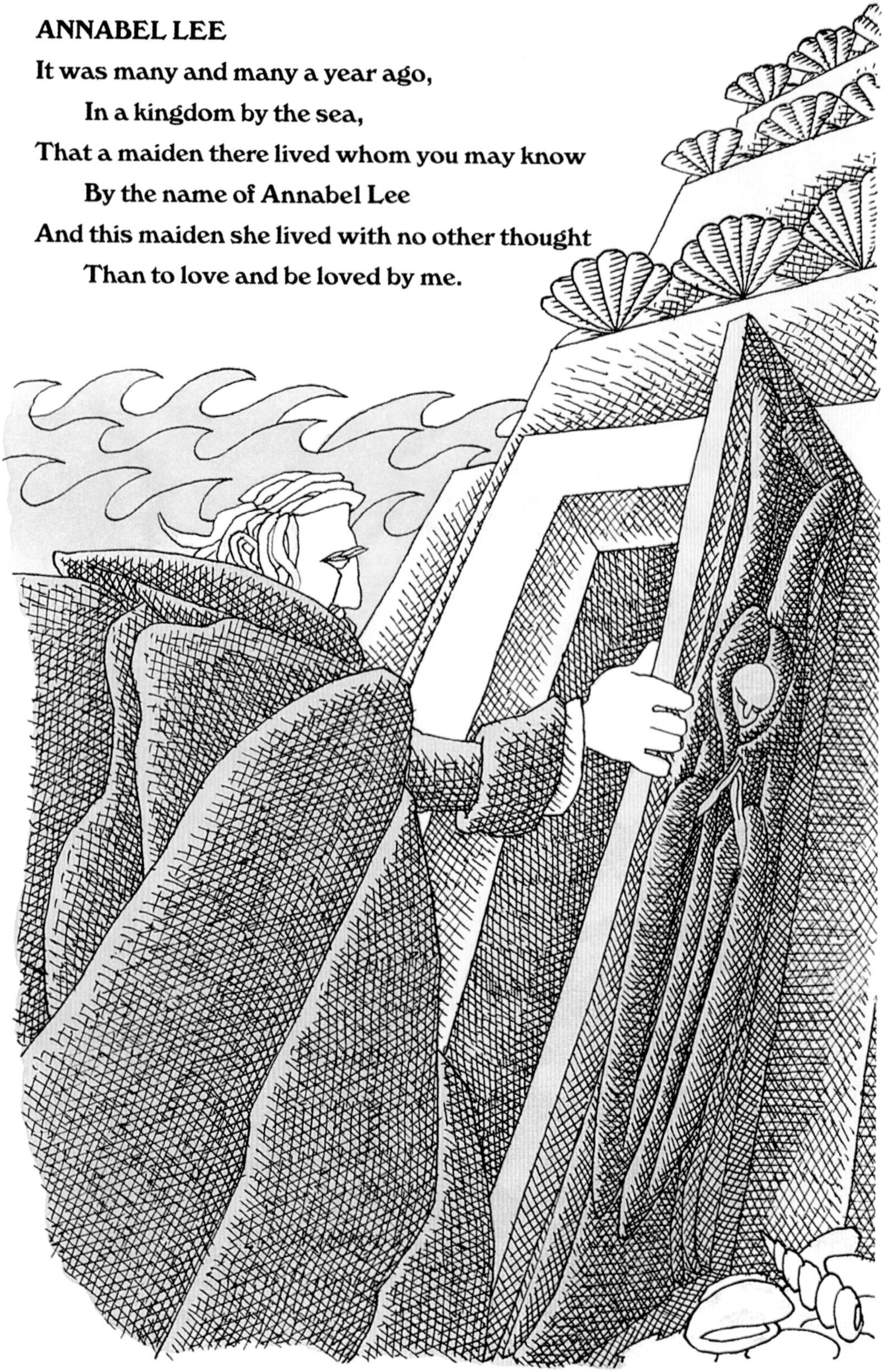

I was a child and she was a child,
    In this kingdom by the sea;
But we loved with a love that was more than love—
    I and my Annabel Lee;
With a love that the wingèd seraphs of heaven
    Coveted her and me.

And this was the reason that, long ago,
    In this kingdom by the sea,
A wind blew out of a cloud, chilling
    My beautiful Annabel Lee;
So that her highborn kinsman came
    And bore her away from me,
To shut her up in a sepulchre
    In this kingdom by the sea.

The angels, not half so happy in heaven,
    Went envying her and me—
Yes!— that was the reason (as all men know,
    In this kingdom by the sea)
That the wind came out of the cloud by night,
    Chilling and killing my Annabel Lee.

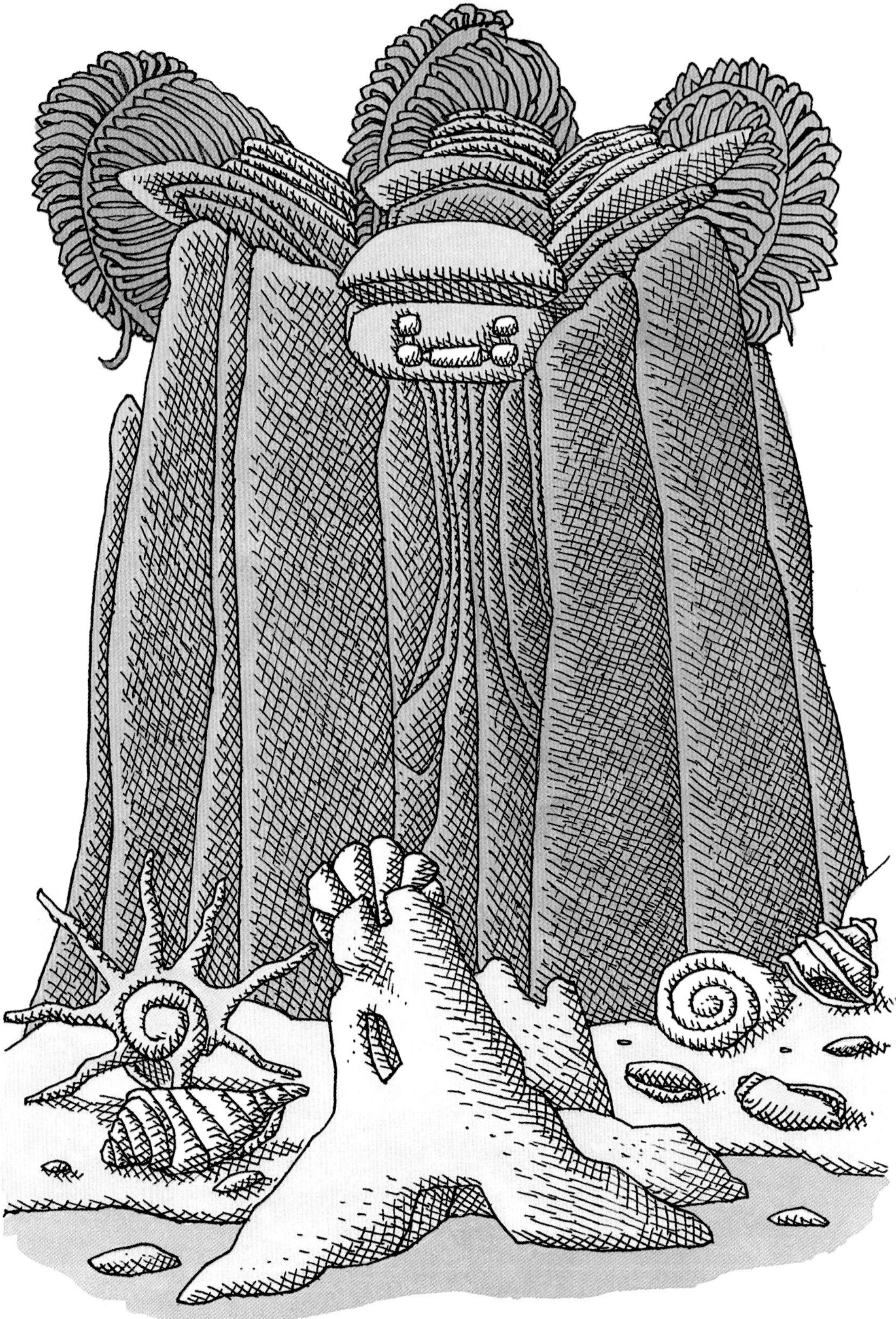

But our love it was stronger by far than the love
    Of those who were older than we—
    Of many far wiser than we—
And neither the angels in heaven above,
    Nor the demons down under the sea,
Can ever dissever my soul from the soul
    Of the beautiful Annabel Lee.
For the moon never beams
    without bringing me dreams
    Of the beautiful Annabel Lee;
And the stars never rise but I feel the bright eyes
    Of the beautiful Annabel Lee;

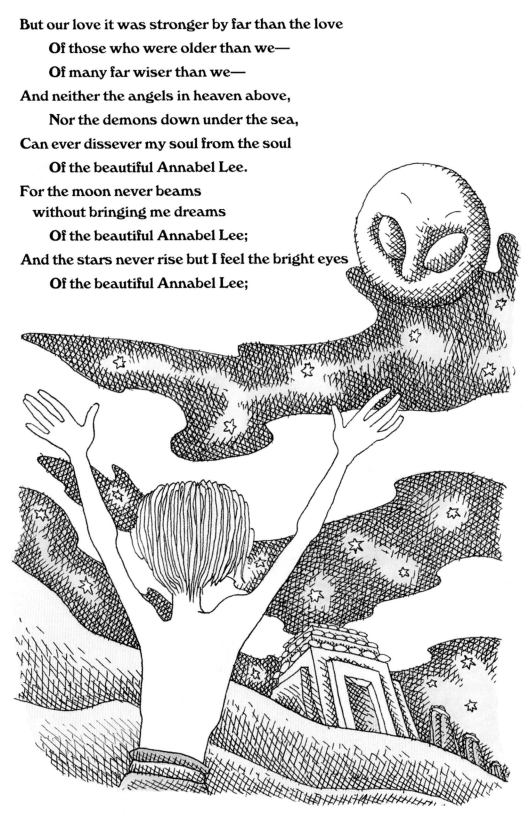

And so, all the night-tide, I lie down by the side
Of my darling— my darling— my life and my bride,
In the sepulchre there by the sea,
In her tomb by the sounding sea.

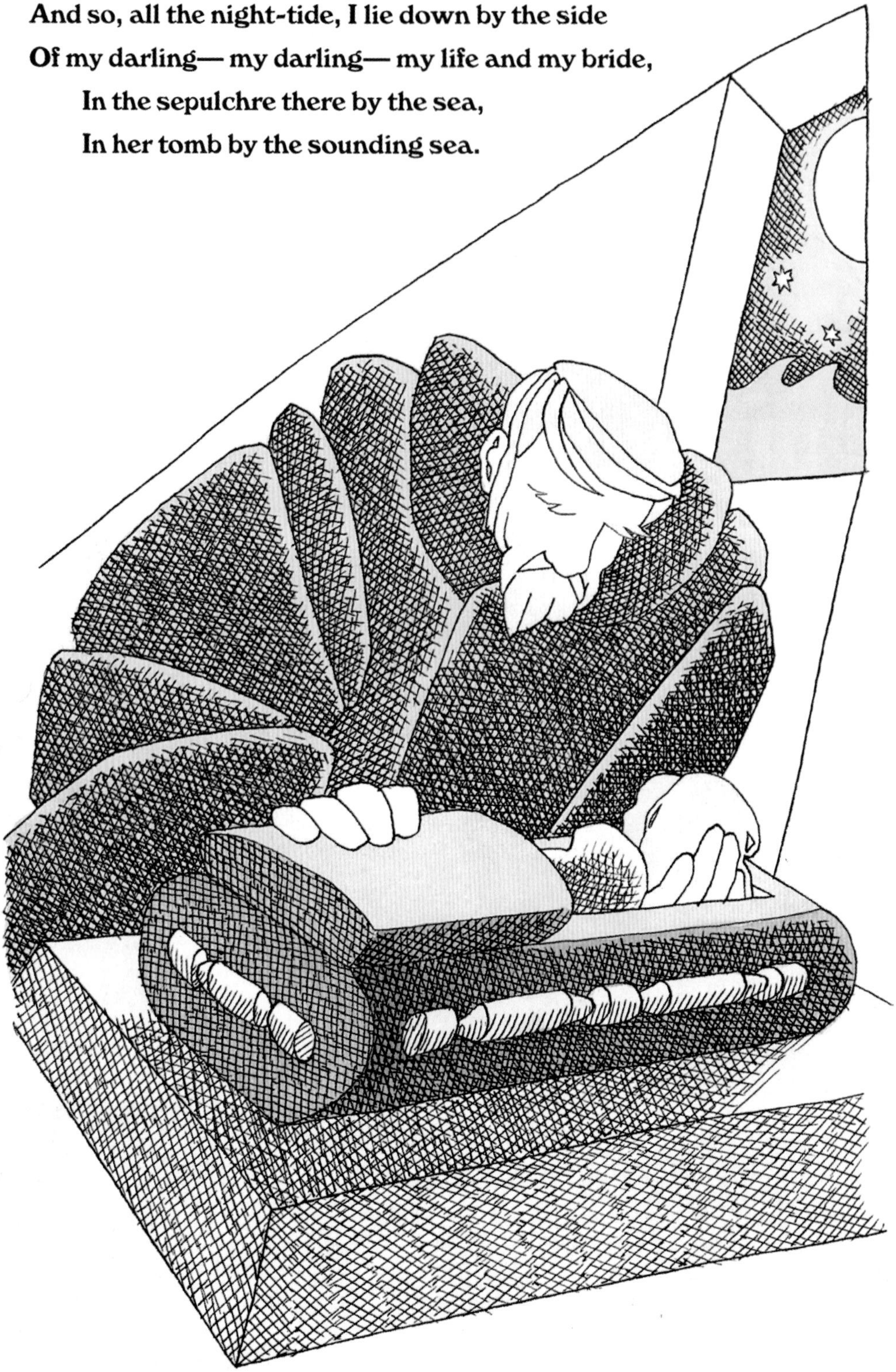

LINES ON ALE

Fill with mingled cream and amber,
    I will drain that glass again.
Such hilarious visions clamber
    Through the chamber of my brain—
Quaintest thoughts— queerest fancies
    Come to life and fade away;
What care I how time advances?
    I am drinking ale today.

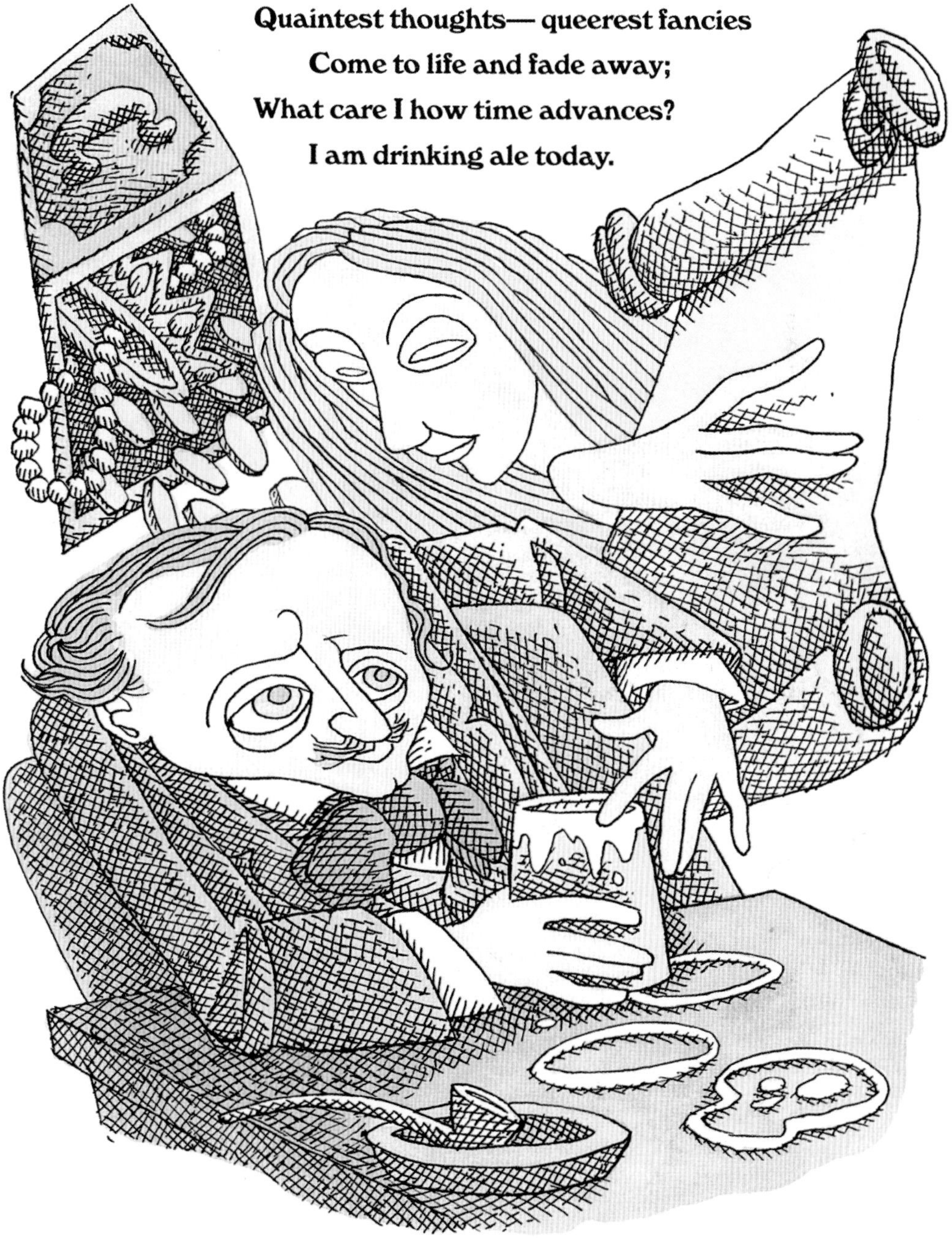

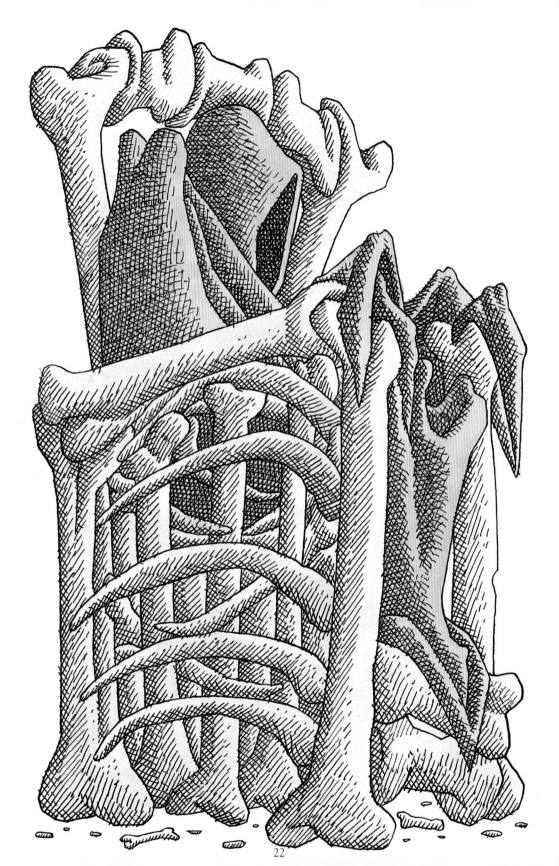

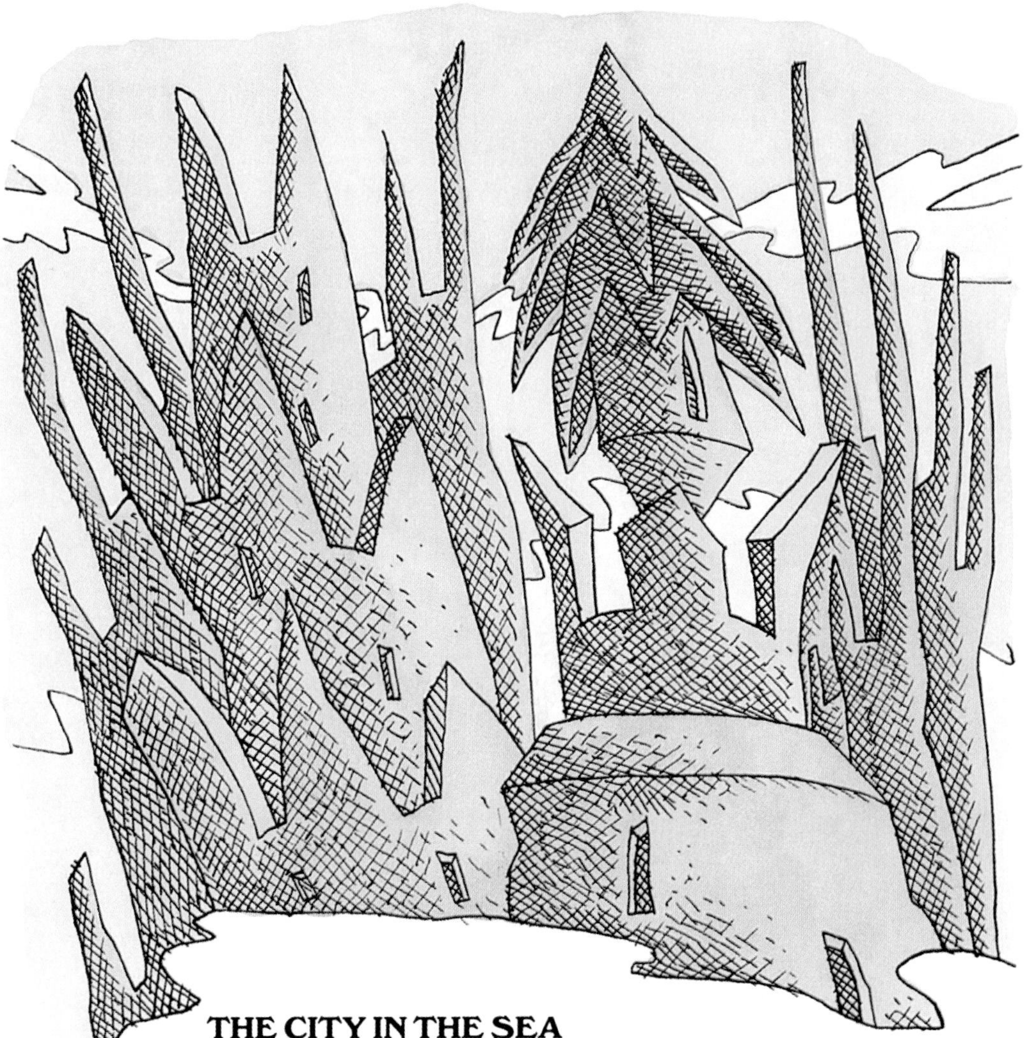

THE CITY IN THE SEA

Lo! Death has reared himself a throne
In a strange city lying alone
Far down within the dim West
Where the good and the bad and the worst and the best
Have gone to their eternal rest.
There shrines and palaces and towers
(Time-eaten towers that tremble not!)
Resemble nothing that is ours.
Around, by lifting winds forgot,
Resignedly beneath the sky
The melancholy waters lie.

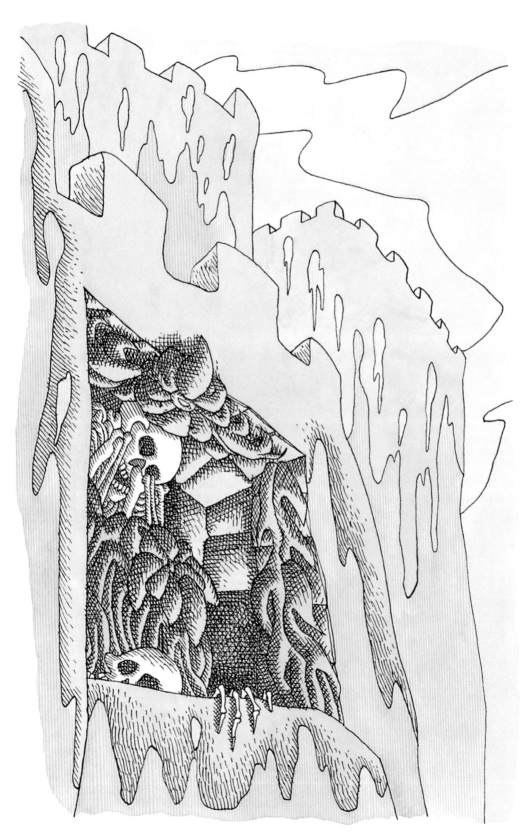

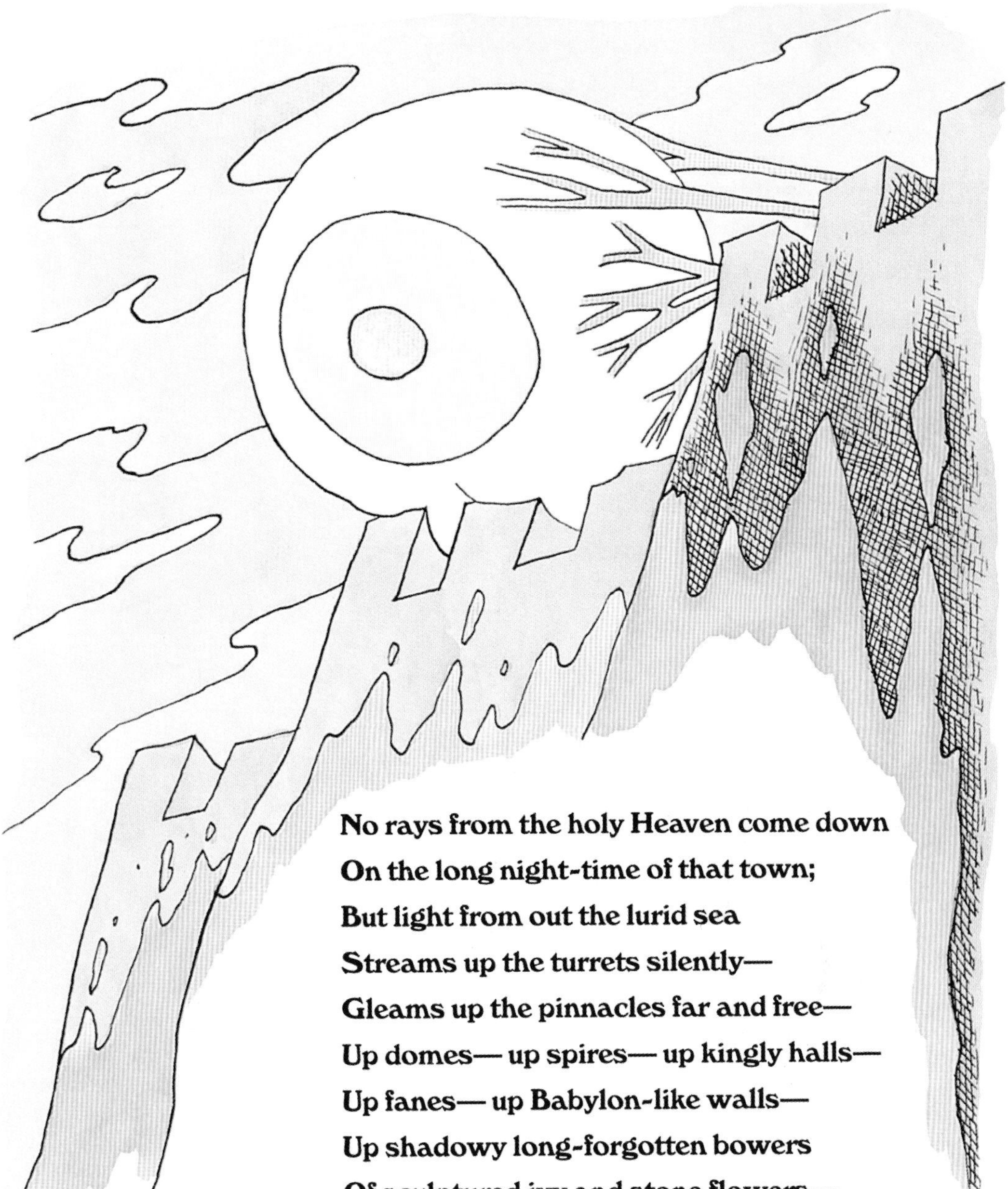

No rays from the holy Heaven come down
On the long night-time of that town;
But light from out the lurid sea
Streams up the turrets silently—
Gleams up the pinnacles far and free—
Up domes— up spires— up kingly halls—
Up fanes— up Babylon-like walls—
Up shadowy long-forgotten bowers
Of sculptured ivy and stone flowers—
Up many and many a marvellous shrine
Whose wreathèd friezes intertwine
The viol, the violet, and the vine.
Resignedly beneath the sky
The melancholy waters lie.
So blend the turrets and shadows there
That all seem pendulous in air,
While from a proud tower in the town

There open fanes and gaping graves
Yawn level with the luminous waves;
But not the riches there that lie
In each idol's diamond eye—
Not the gayly-jewelled dead
Tempt the waters from their bed;
For no ripples curl, alas!
Along that wilderness of glass—
No swellings tell that winds may be
Upon some far-off happier sea—
No heavings hint that winds have been
On seas less hideously serene.

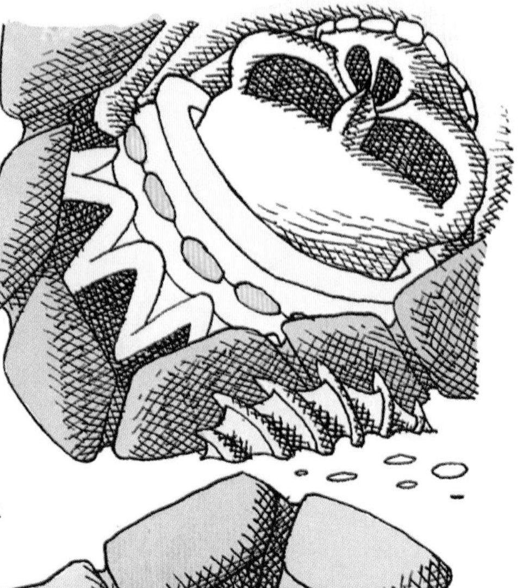

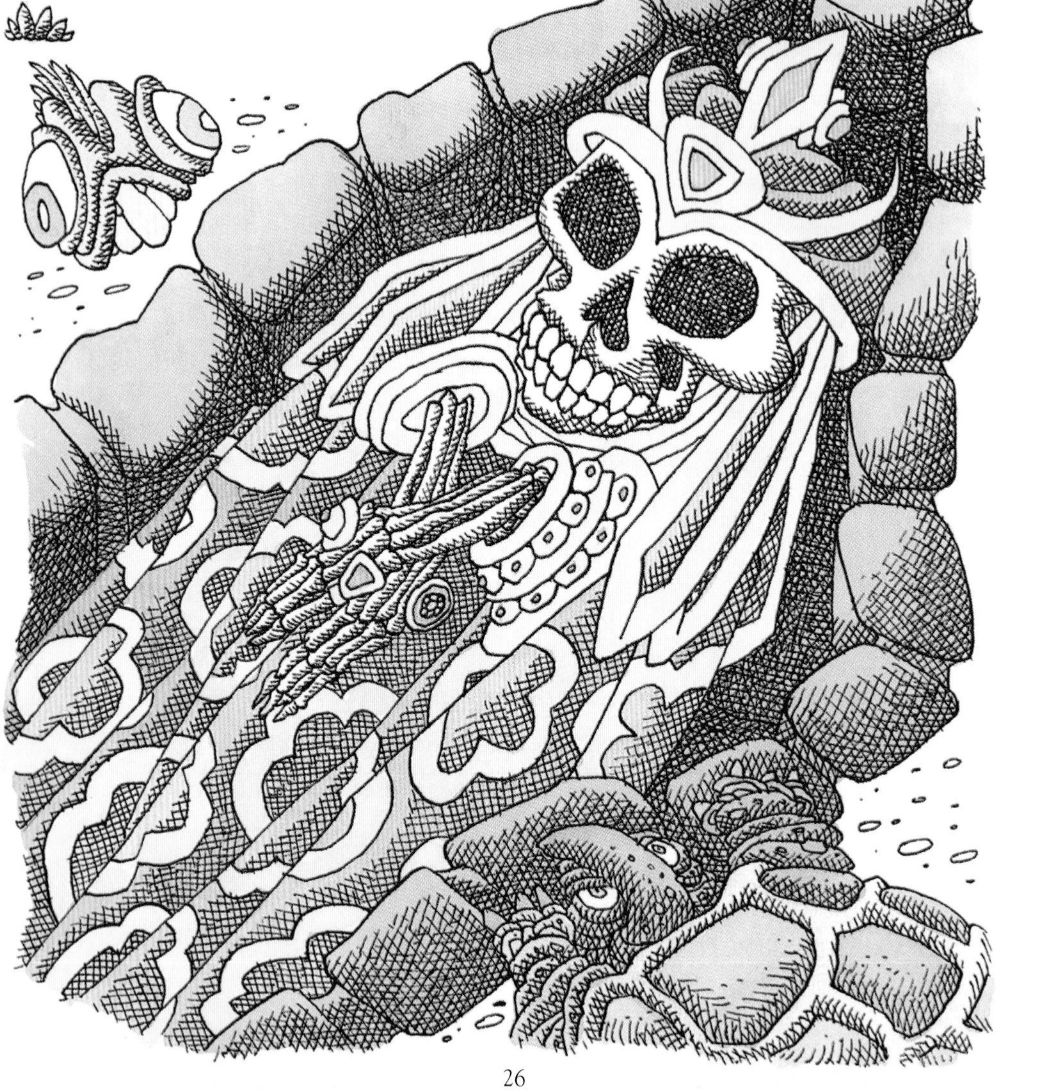

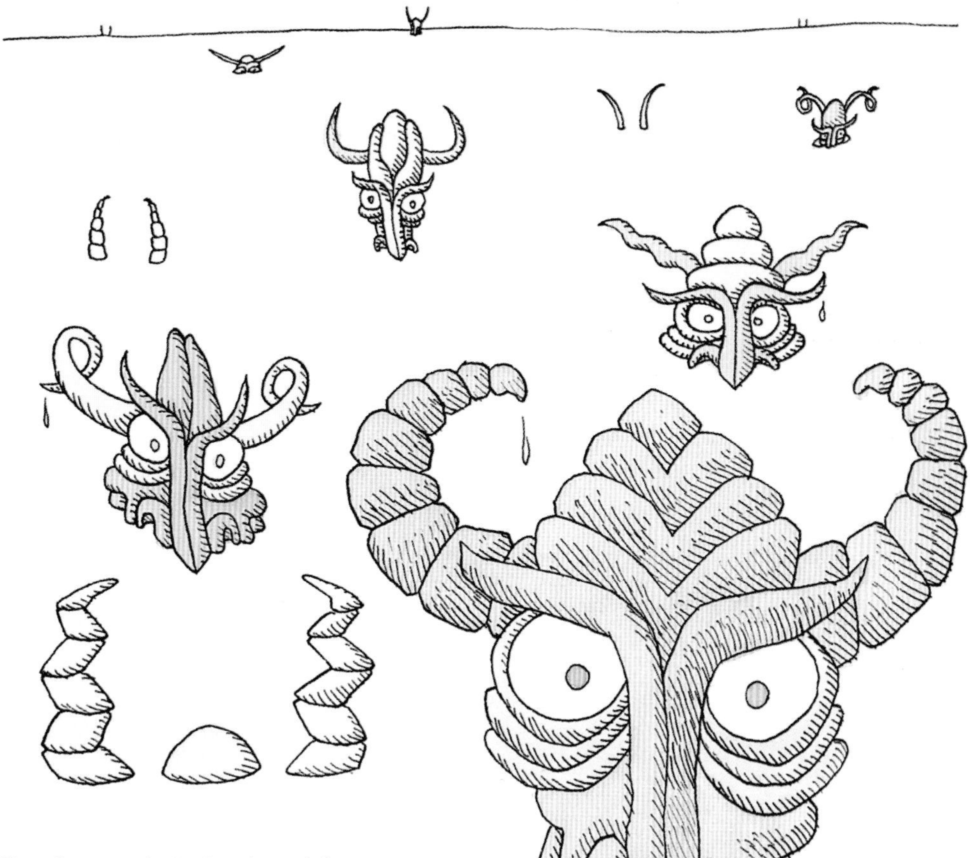

But lo, a stir is in the air!
The wave— there is a movement there!
As if the towers had thrust aside,
In slightly sinking, the dull tide—
As if their tops had feebly given
A void within the filmy Heaven.
The waves have now a redder glow—
The hours are breathing faint and low—
And when, amid no earthly moans,
Down, down that town shall settle hence,
Hell, rising from a thousand thrones,
Shall do it reverence.

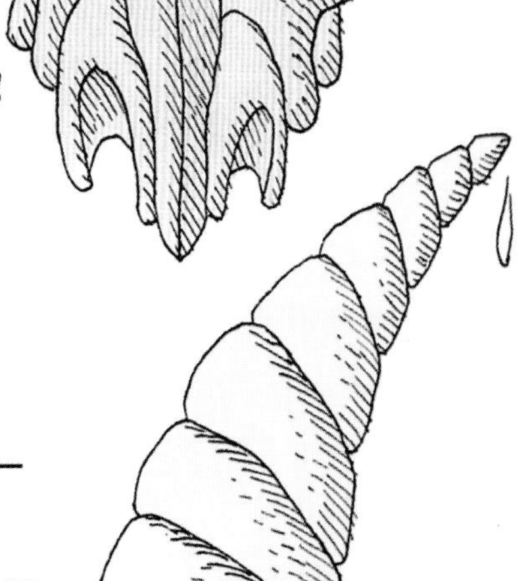

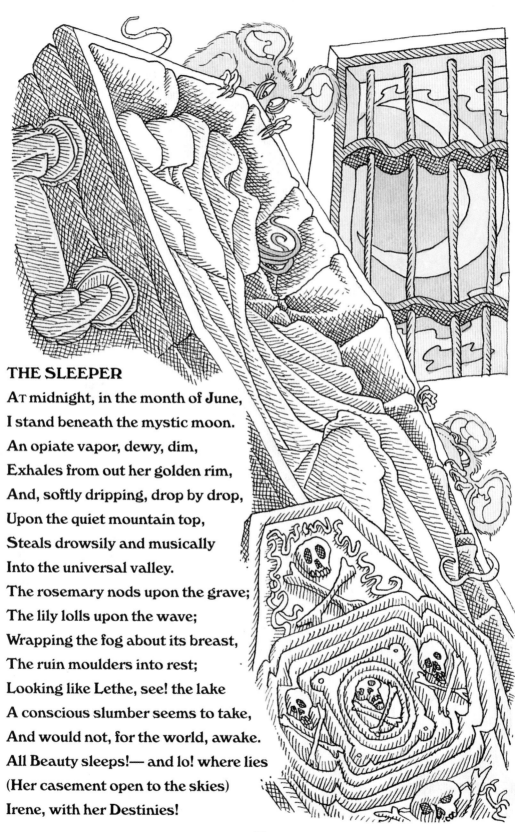

THE SLEEPER

At midnight, in the month of June,
I stand beneath the mystic moon.
An opiate vapor, dewy, dim,
Exhales from out her golden rim,
And, softly dripping, drop by drop,
Upon the quiet mountain top,
Steals drowsily and musically
Into the universal valley.
The rosemary nods upon the grave;
The lily lolls upon the wave;
Wrapping the fog about its breast,
The ruin moulders into rest;
Looking like Lethe, see! the lake
A conscious slumber seems to take,
And would not, for the world, awake.
All Beauty sleeps!— and lo! where lies
(Her casement open to the skies)
Irene, with her Destinies!

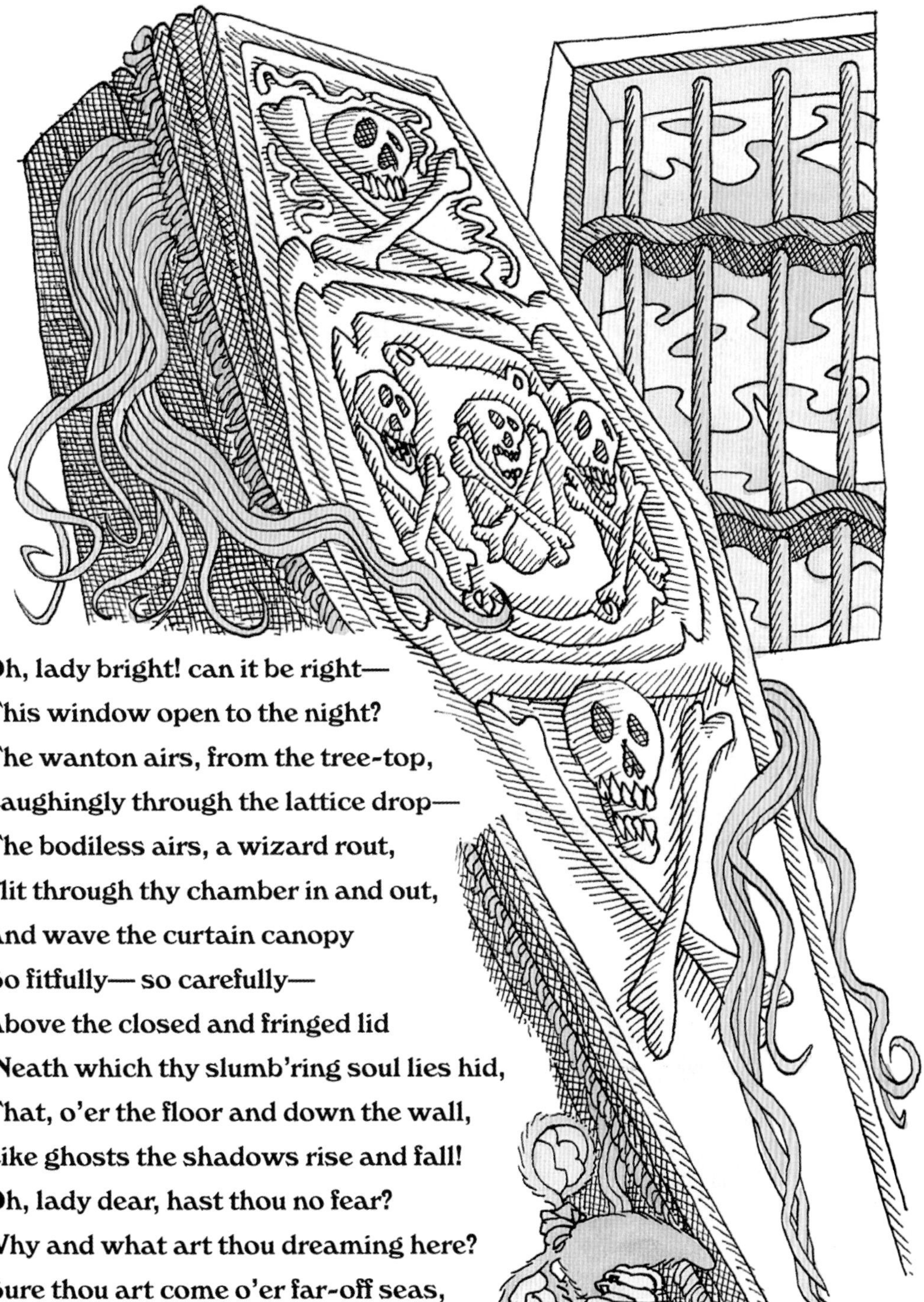

Oh, lady bright! can it be right—
This window open to the night?
The wanton airs, from the tree-top,
Laughingly through the lattice drop—
The bodiless airs, a wizard rout,
Flit through thy chamber in and out,
And wave the curtain canopy
So fitfully— so carefully—
Above the closed and fringed lid
'Neath which thy slumb'ring soul lies hid,
That, o'er the floor and down the wall,
Like ghosts the shadows rise and fall!
Oh, lady dear, hast thou no fear?
Why and what art thou dreaming here?
Sure thou art come o'er far-off seas,
A wonder to these garden trees!
Strange is thy pallor! strange thy dress!
Strange, above all, thy length of tress,
And this all solemn silentness!

The lady sleeps! Oh, may her sleep,
Which is enduring, so be deep!
Heaven have her in its sacred keep!
This chamber changed for one more holy,
This bed for one more melancholy,
I pray to God that she may lie
Forever with unopened eye,
While the dim sheeted ghosts go by!

My love, she sleeps! Oh, may her sleep,
As it is lasting, so be deep!
Soft may the worms about her creep!
Far in the forest, dim and old,
For her may some tall vault unfold—
Some vault that oft hath flung its black
And winged panels fluttering back,
Triumphant, o'er the crested palls,
Of her grand family funerals—
Some sepulchre, remote, alone,
Against whose portal she hath thrown,
In childhood, many an idle stone—
Some tomb from out whose sounding door
She ne'er shall force an echo more,
Thrilling to think, poor child of sin!
It was the dead who groaned within.

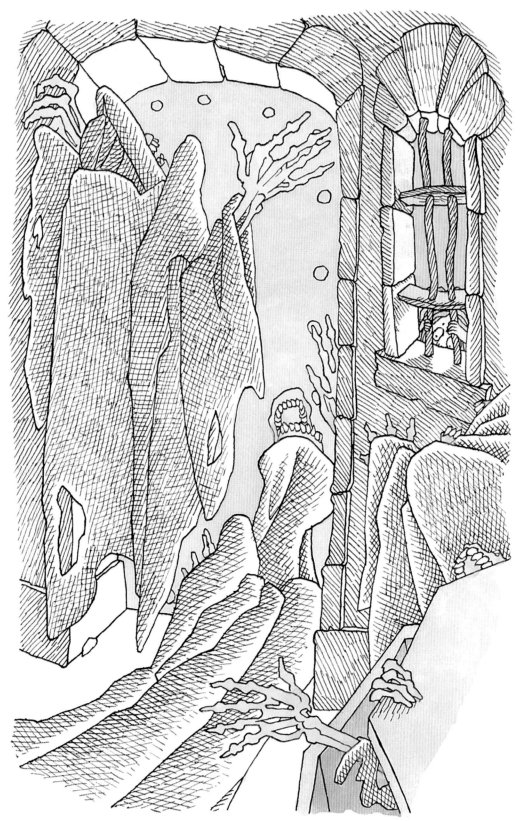

ELDORADO

Gaily bedight,
A gallant knight,
In sunshine and in shadow,
Had journeyed long,
Singing a song,
In search of Eldorado.

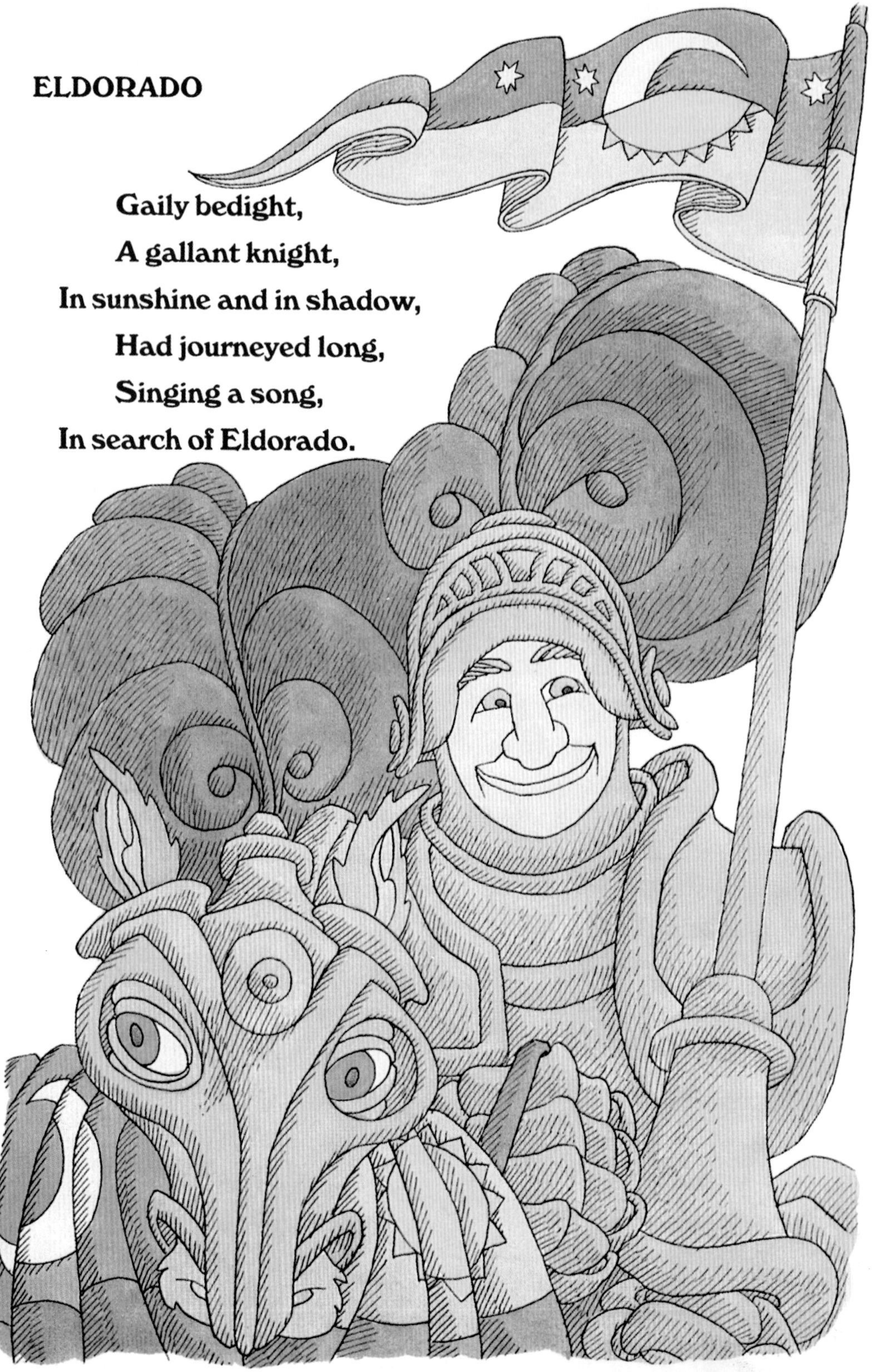

But he grew old—
This knight so bold—
And o'er his heart a shadow
Fell as he found
No spot of ground
That looked like Eldorado.

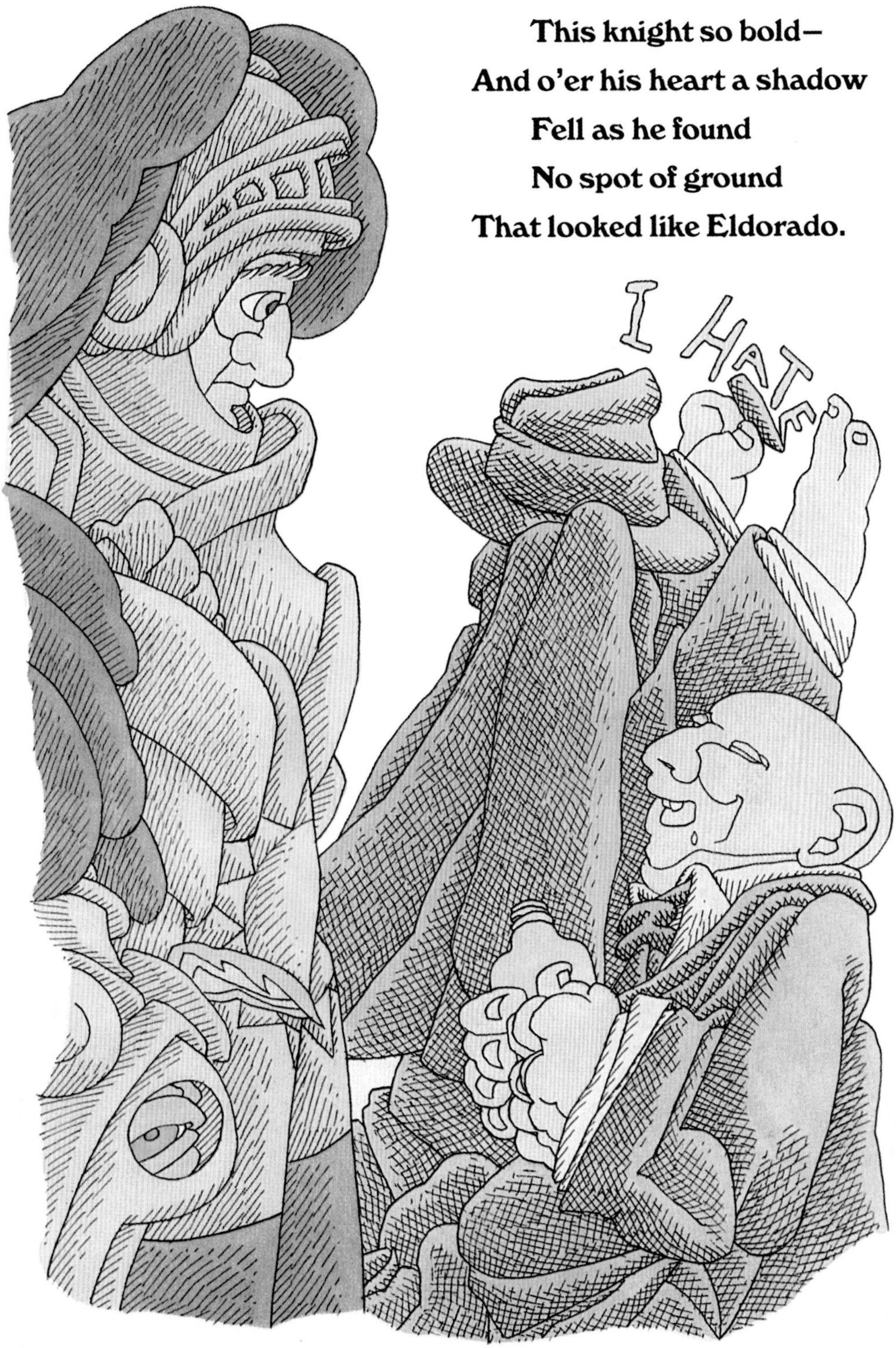
I HATE

And, as his strength
Failed him at length,
He met a pilgrim shadow–
"Shadow," said he,
"Where can it be–
This land of Eldorado?"

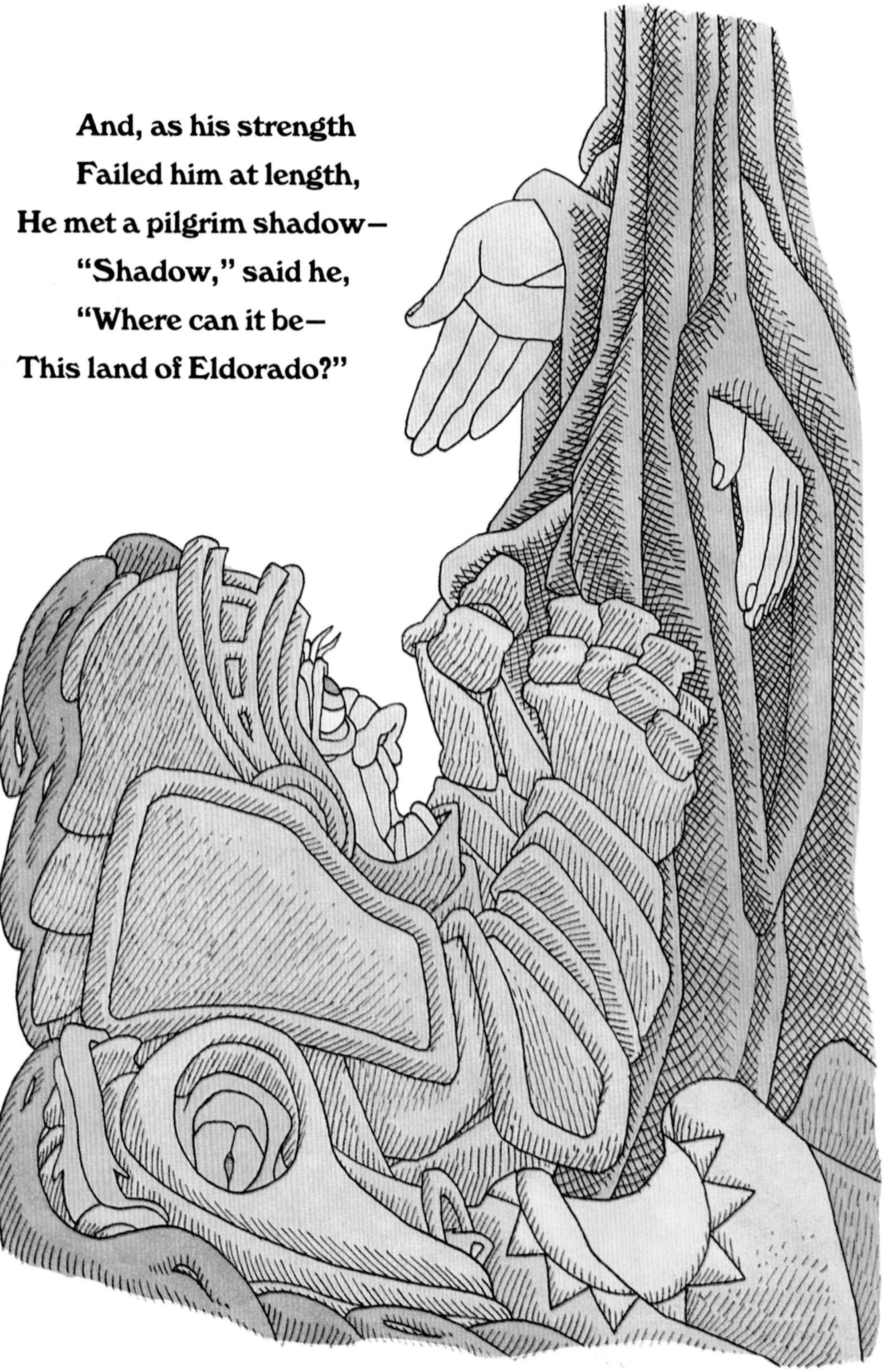

"Over the Mountains
Of the Moon,
Down the Valley of the Shadow,
Ride, boldly ride,"
The shade replied—
"If you seek for Eldorado!"

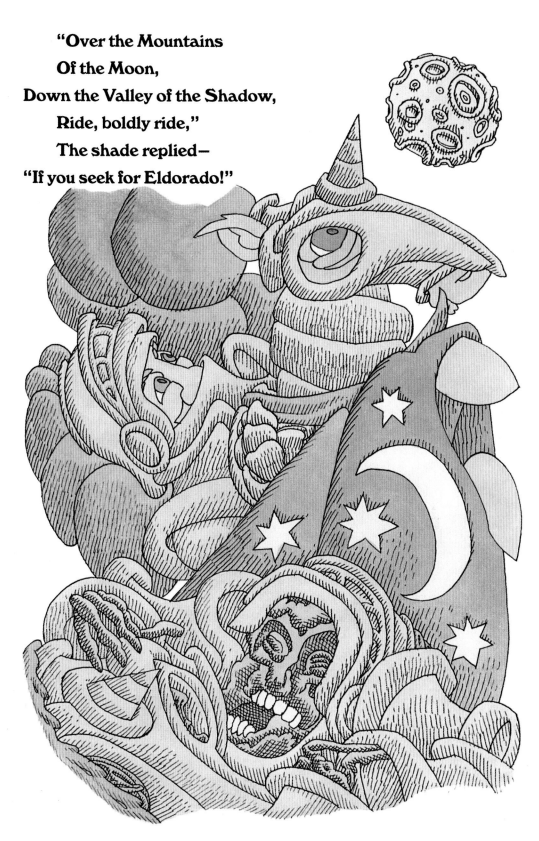

ALONE

FROM childhood's hour I have not been
As others were— I have not seen
As others saw— I could not bring
My passions from a common spring.
From the same source I have not taken
My sorrow; I could not awaken
My heart to joy at the same tone;
And all I lov'd, *I* lov'd alone.

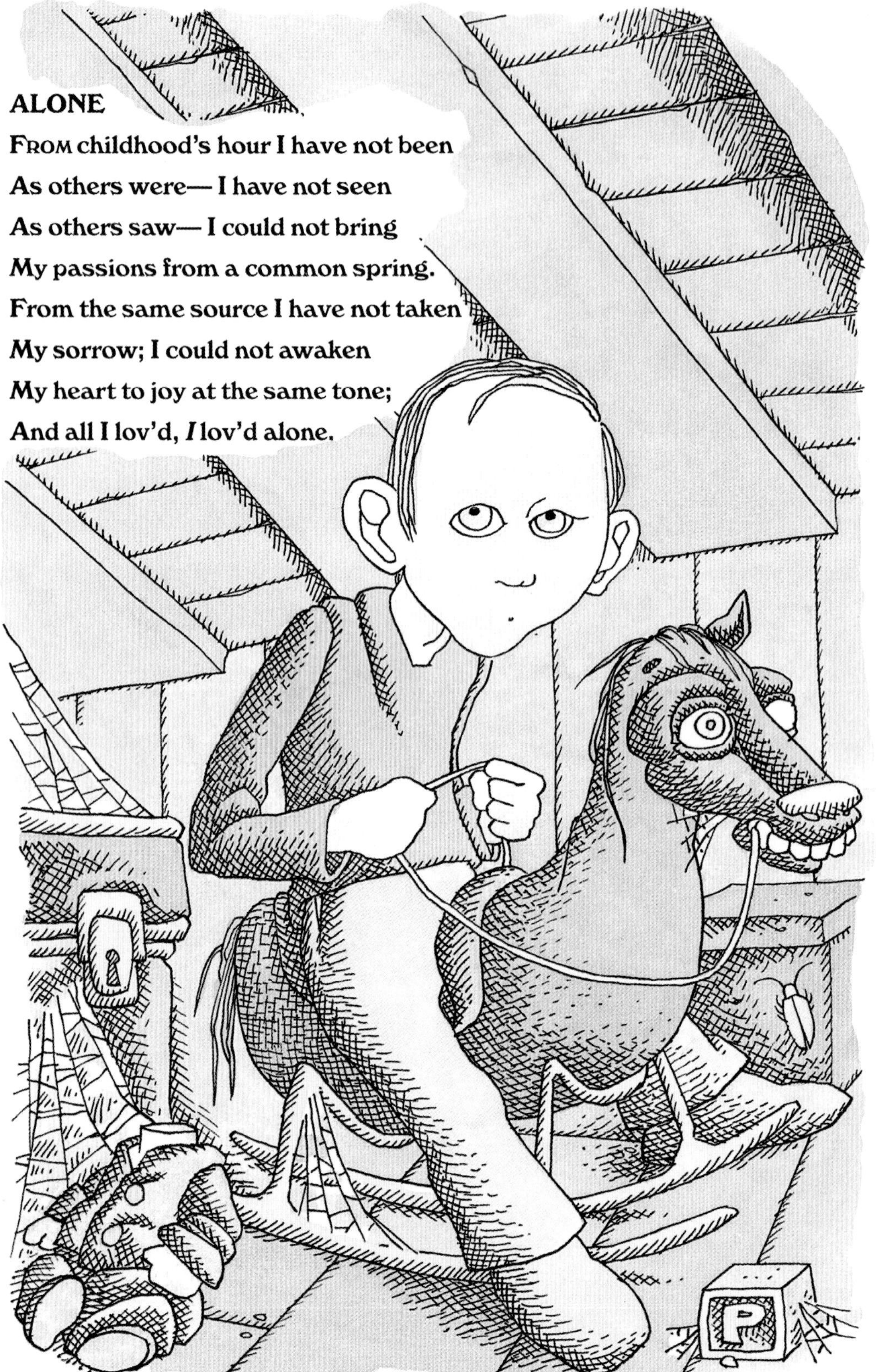
P

Then— in my childhood— in the dawn
Of a most stormy life— was drawn
From ev'ry depth of good and ill
The mystery which binds me still:
From the torrent, or the fountain,
From the red cliff of the mountain,
From the sun that 'round me roll'd
In its autumn tint of gold—
From the lightning in the sky
As it pass'd me flying by—
From the thunder and the storm,
And the cloud that took the form
(When the rest of Heaven was blue)
Of a demon in my view.

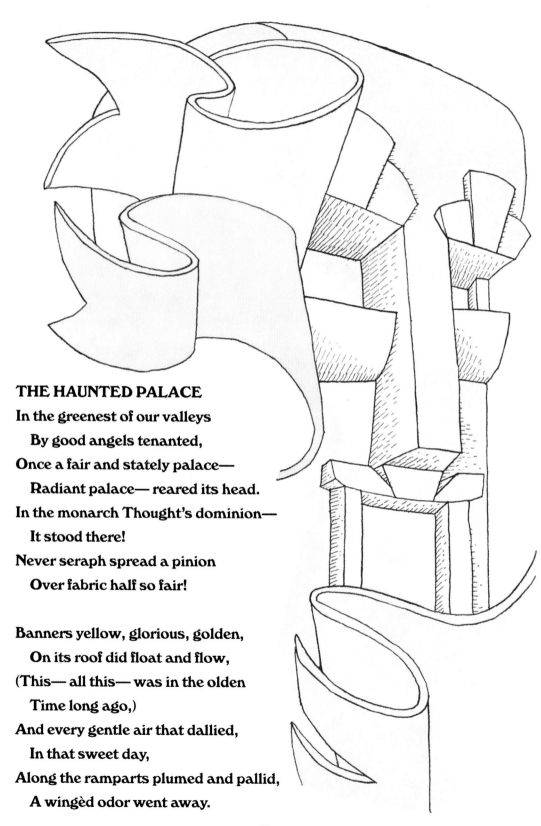

THE HAUNTED PALACE

In the greenest of our valleys
 By good angels tenanted,
Once a fair and stately palace—
 Radiant palace— reared its head.
In the monarch Thought's dominion—
 It stood there!
Never seraph spread a pinion
 Over fabric half so fair!

Banners yellow, glorious, golden,
 On its roof did float and flow,
(This— all this— was in the olden
 Time long ago,)
And every gentle air that dallied,
 In that sweet day,
Along the ramparts plumed and pallid,
 A wingèd odor went away.

Wanderers in that happy valley,
    Through two luminous windows, saw
Spirits moving musically,
    To a lute's well tunèd law,
Round about a throne where, sitting
    (Porphyrogene!)
In state his glory well befitting,
    The ruler of the realm was seen.

And all with pearl and ruby glowing
    Was the fair palace-door,
Through which came flowing, flowing, flowing,
    And sparkling evermore,
A troop of Echoes, whose sweet duty
    Was but to sing,
In voices of surpassing beauty,
    The wit and wisdom of their king.

But evil things, in robes of sorrow,
    Assailed the monarch's high estate.
(Ah, let us mourn!— for never morrow
    Shall dawn upon him desolate!)
And round about his home, the glory
    That blushed and bloomed
Is but a dim-remembered story
    Of the old time entombed.

And travellers now, within that valley,
    Through the red-litten windows see
Vast forms, that move fantastically
    To a discordant melody,
While, like a ghastly rapid river,
    Through the pale door
A hideous throng rush out forever
    And laugh— but smile no more.

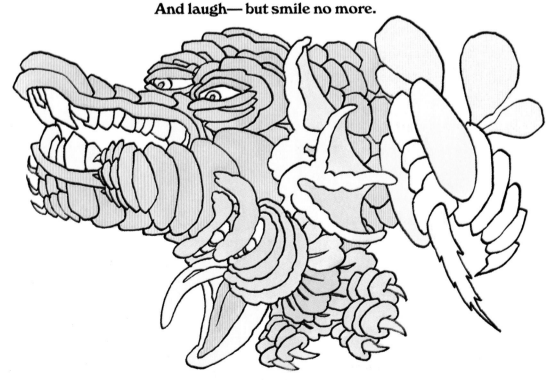

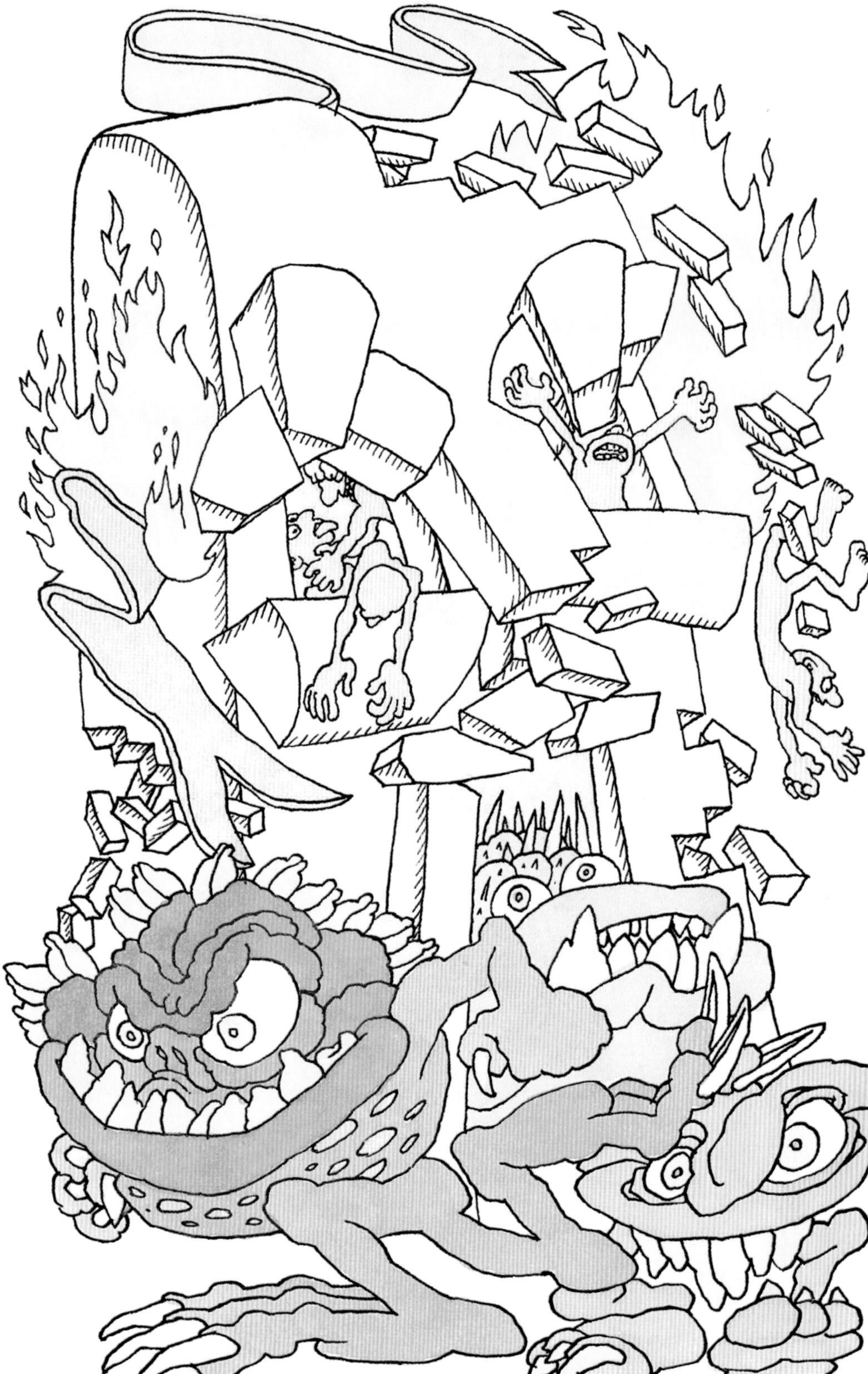

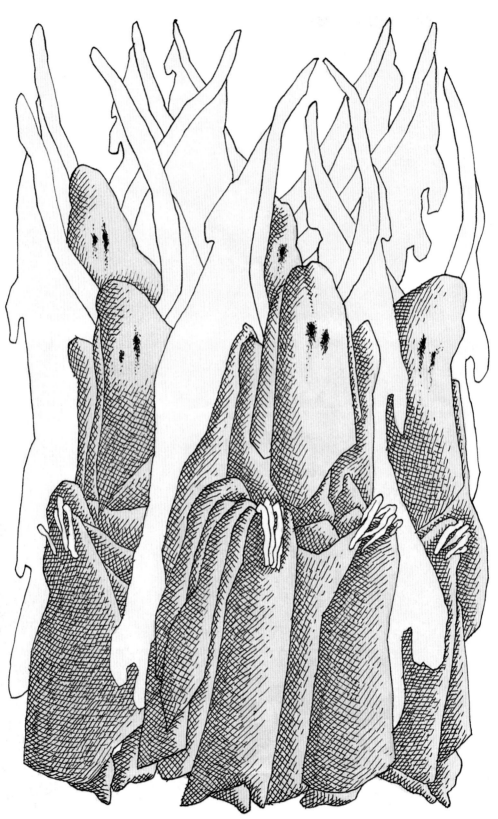

THE CONQUEROR WORM

Lo! 'tis a gala night
  Within the lonesome latter years!
An angel throng, bewinged, bedight
  In veils, and drowned in tears,
Sit in a theatre, to see
  A play of hopes and fears,
While the orchestra breathes fitfully
  The music of the spheres.

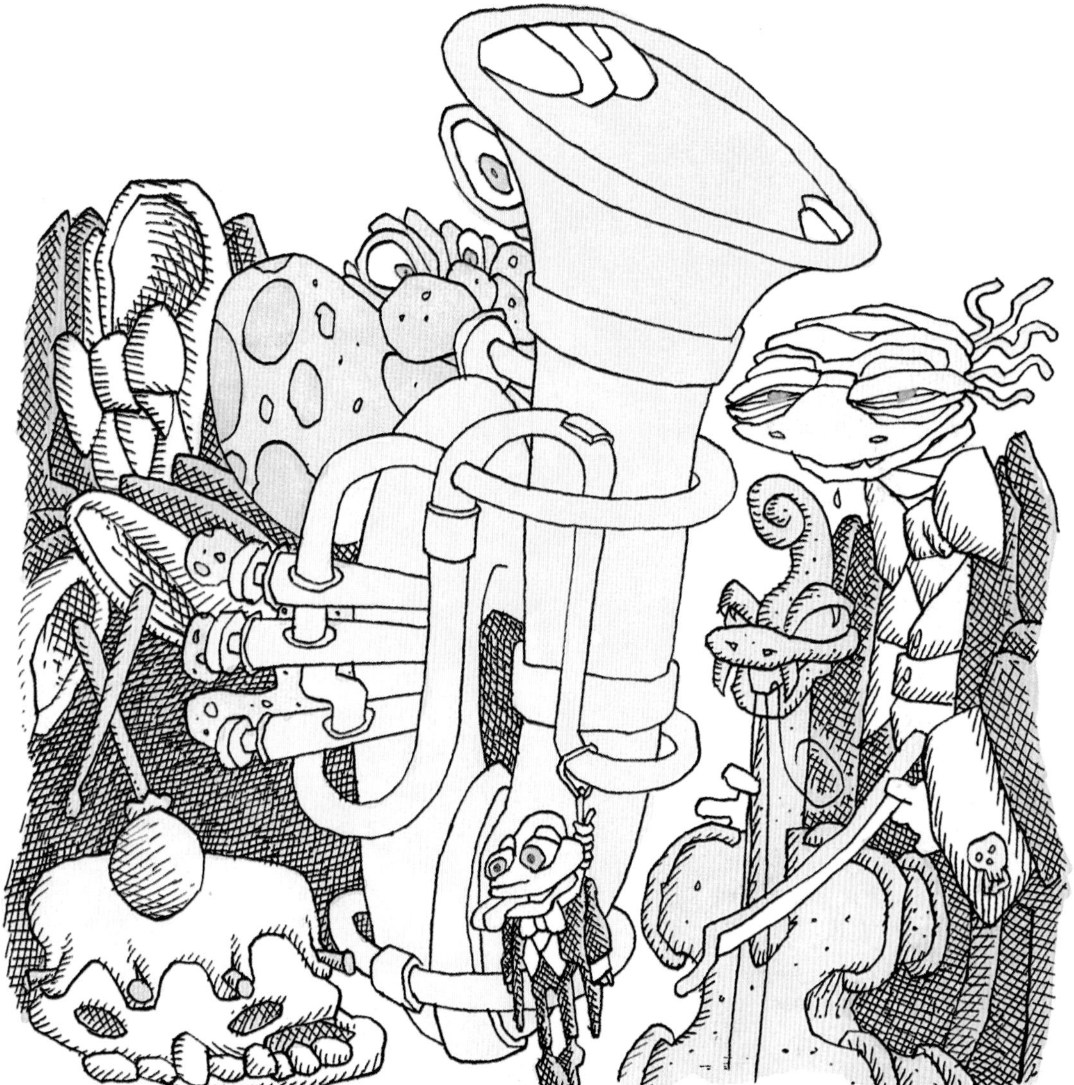

Mimes, in the form of God on high,
  Mutter and mumble low,
And hither and thither fly—
  Mere puppets they, who come and go
At bidding of vast formless things
  That shift the scenery to and fro,
Flapping from out their Condor wings
  Invisible Woe!

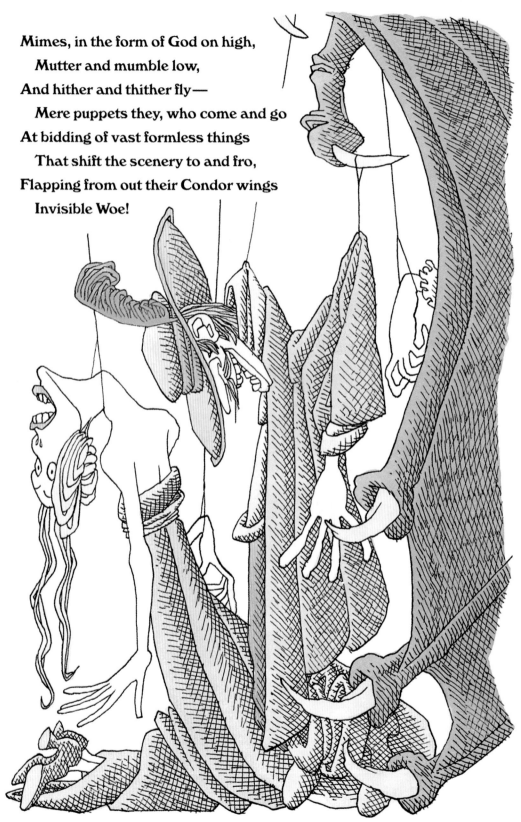

That motley drama—oh, be sure
  It shall not be forgot!
With its Phantom chased for evermore,
  By a crowd that seize it not,
Through a circle that ever returneth in
  To the self-same spot,
And much of Madness, and more of Sin,
  And Horror the soul of the plot.

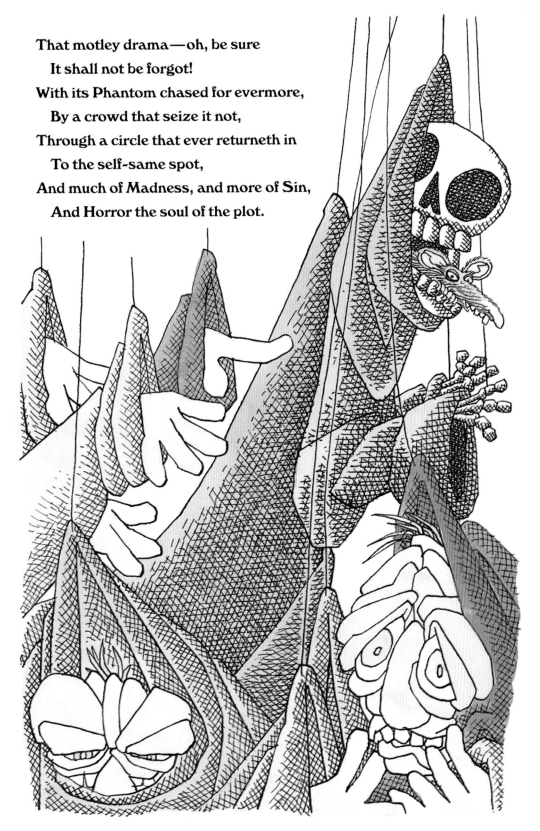

But see, amid the mimic rout
    A crawling shape intrude!
A blood-red thing that writhes from out
    The scenic solitude!
It writhes!—it writhes!—with mortal pangs
    The mimes become its food,
And the angels sob at vermin fangs
    In human gore imbued.

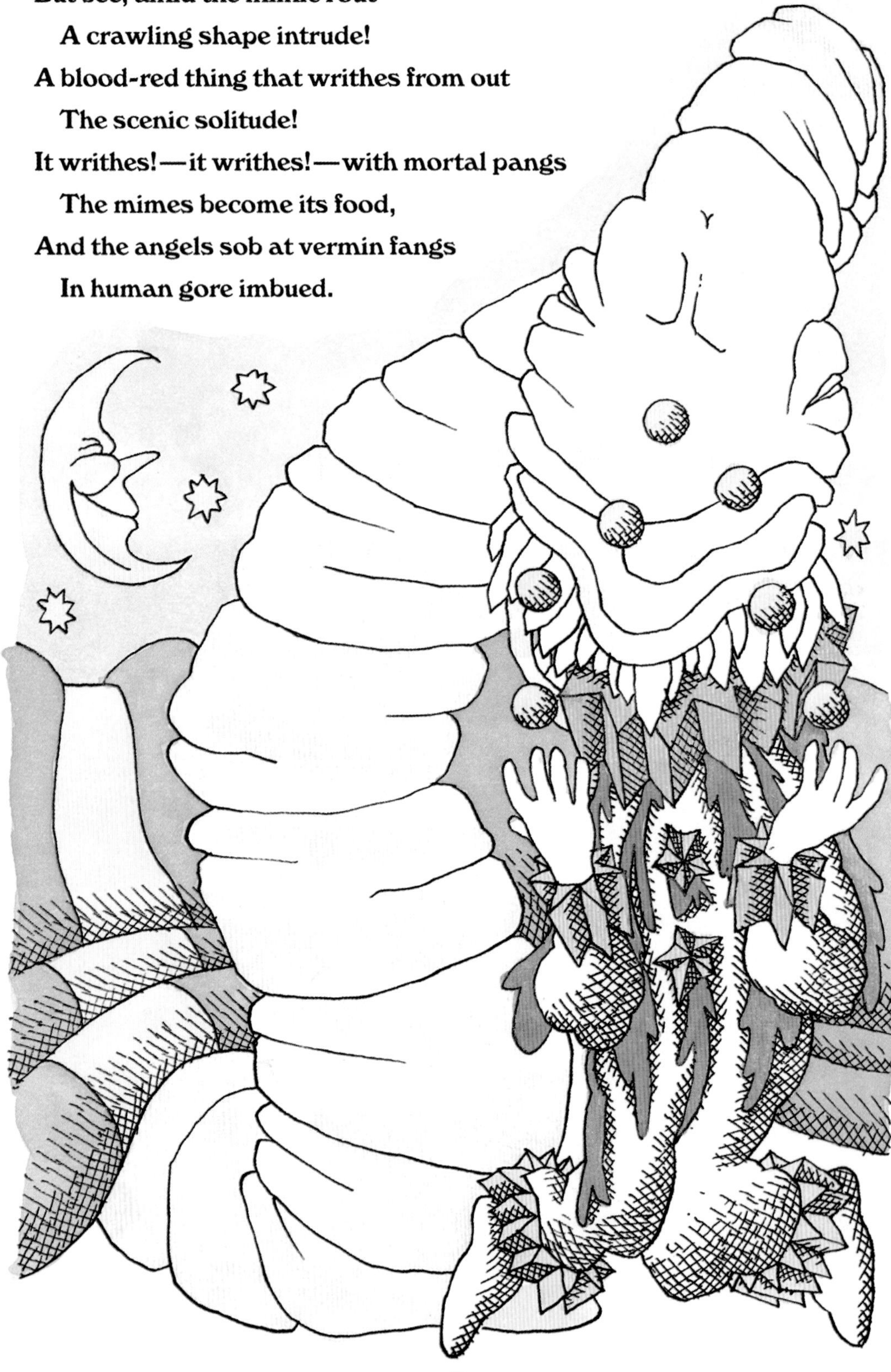

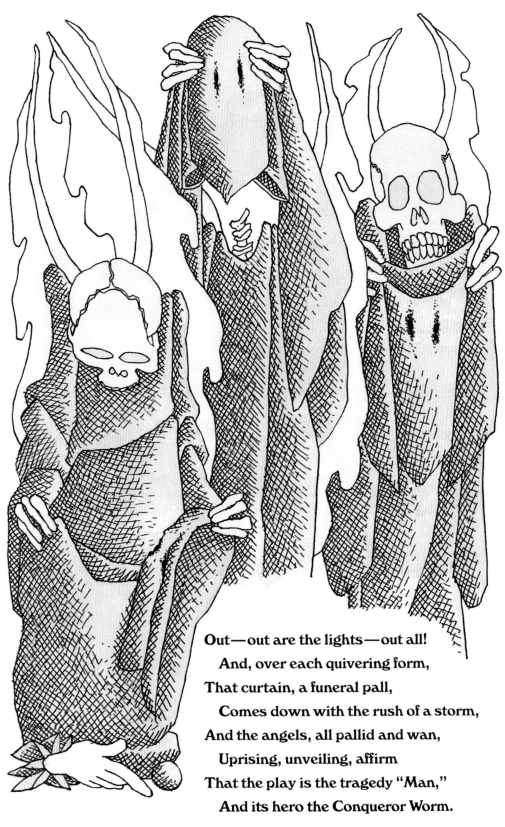

Out—out are the lights—out all!
  And, over each quivering form,
That curtain, a funeral pall,
  Comes down with the rush of a storm,
And the angels, all pallid and wan,
  Uprising, unveiling, affirm
That the play is the tragedy "Man,"
  And its hero the Conqueror Worm.

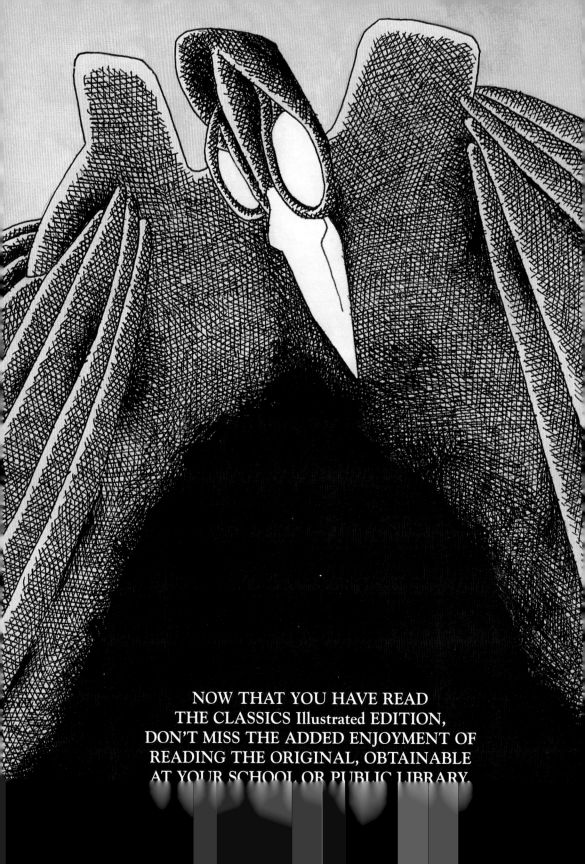

NOW THAT YOU HAVE READ
THE CLASSICS Illustrated EDITION,
DON'T MISS THE ADDED ENJOYMENT OF
READING THE ORIGINAL, OBTAINABLE
AT YOUR SCHOOL OR PUBLIC LIBRARY.

WATCH OUT FOR
PAPERCUTZ™

Welcome to the fourth Papercutz edition of CLASSICS ILLUSTRATED. I'm Jim Salicrup, Papercutz Editor-in Chief, and still proud to be part of this exciting revival of one of the world's most well-known and successful comics series.

We're especially proud to present in this edition the classic poems by Edgar Allan Poe illustrated by the legendary cartoonist Gahan Wilson. Not long ago, the Museum of Comic and Cartoon Art honored Mr. Wilson with a special award at one of their annual Art Fests. Being a Trustee for MoCCA, I couldn't resist taking advantage of the opportunity to ask Mr. Wilson if he'd being willing to draw a sketch for me. Well, the result was incredible – it's a macabre portrait of me, sort of exaggerating the lengths I'll go to to help raise much-needed funds for MoCCA! (For more information go to www.moccany.org.)

If you enjoyed this volume's somewhat frightening features, you may want to check out another world-famous classic comics series, also published by Papercutz – it's TALES FROM THE CRYPT, our revival of the greatest horror comic ever! Every other month we offer up all-new thrills and chills in true TALES FROM THE CRYPT-style, and the stories are all collected in our ongoing series of TALES FROM THE CRYPT graphic novels. Go to www.papercutz.com for a peek at what I'm talking about – if you dare!

On the next few pages, however, we've got another scary treat for you. It's an excerpt from CLASSICS ILLUSTRAT-ED DELUXE #3 "Frankenstein." We think Marion Mousse's adaptation of Mary Shelley's classic novel is truly spectacular, but you can see for yourself on the following pages...

And just to wrap up our spooky plug-fest, CLASSICS ILLUSTRATED #5 features one of the most famous stories featuring a ghost – it's Hamlet by William Shakespeare, adapted by Steven Grant and Tom Mandrake. So, clearly the answer to whether to be here, or not to be here for CLASSICS ILLUSTRATED #5, is be here!

Thanks,

Jim

MAY THE SACRIFICE OF THIS INNOCENT PLEASE THE GODS OF MOCCA!

THE KINDLY HIGH PRIEST CARRYING OUT THE DUTIES OF HIS OFFICE

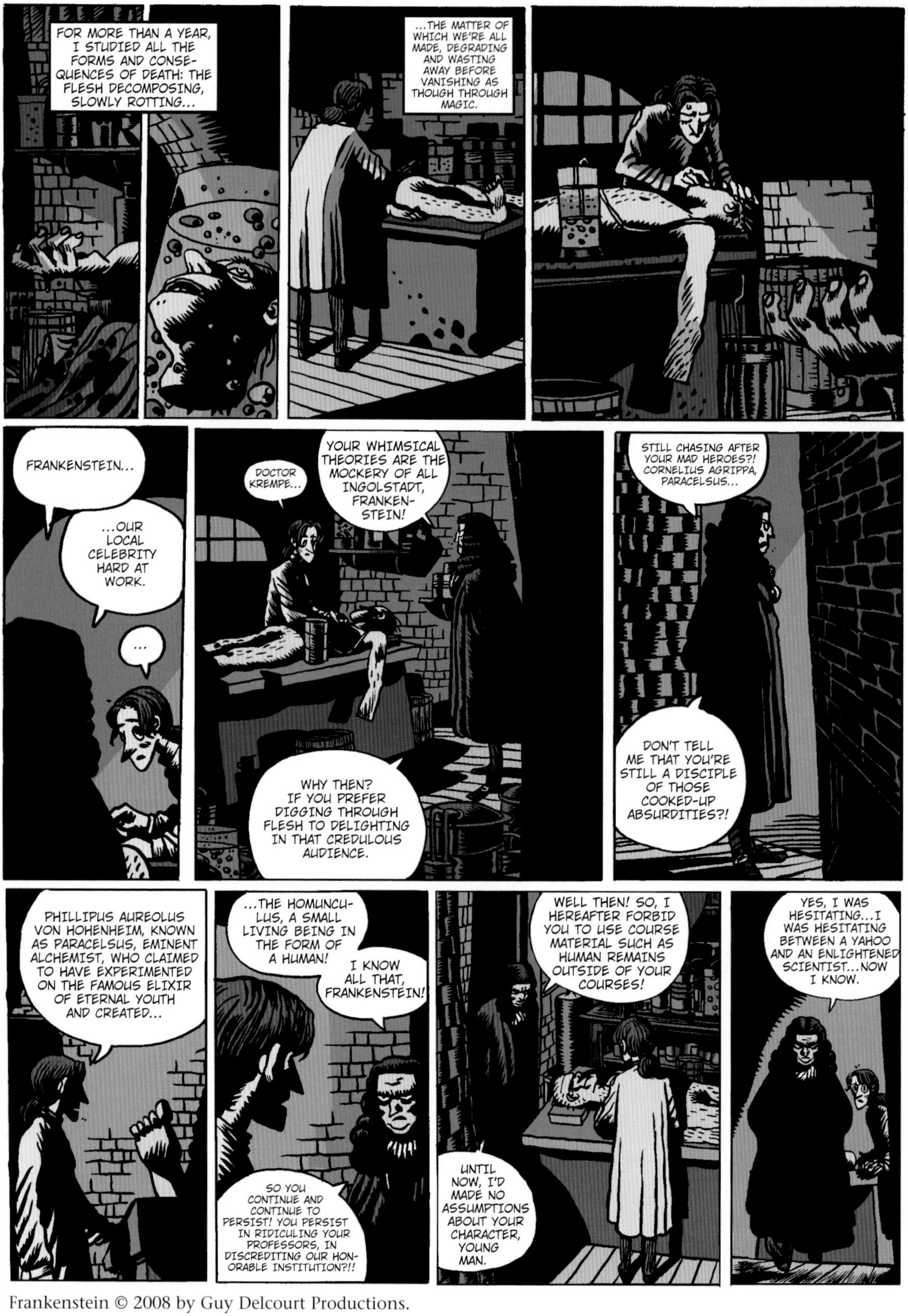
FOR MORE THAN A YEAR, I STUDIED ALL THE FORMS AND CONSE-QUENCES OF DEATH: THE FLESH DECOMPOSING, SLOWLY ROTTING...
...THE MATTER OF WHICH WE'RE ALL MADE, DEGRADING AND WASTING AWAY BEFORE VANISHING AS THOUGH THROUGH MAGIC.
FRANKENSTEIN...
...OUR LOCAL CELEBRITY HARD AT WORK.
...
DOCTOR KREMPE...
YOUR WHIMSICAL THEORIES ARE THE MOCKERY OF ALL INGOLSTADT, FRANKEN-STEIN!
WHY THEN? IF YOU PREFER DIGGING THROUGH FLESH TO DELIGHTING IN THAT CREDULOUS AUDIENCE.
STILL CHASING AFTER YOUR MAD HEROES?! CORNELIUS AGRIPPA, PARACELSUS...
DON'T TELL ME THAT YOU'RE STILL A DISCIPLE OF THOSE COOKED-UP ABSURDITIES?!
PHILLIPUS AUREOLUS VON HOHENHEIM, KNOWN AS PARACELSUS, EMINENT ALCHEMIST, WHO CLAIMED TO HAVE EXPERIMENTED ON THE FAMOUS ELIXIR OF ETERNAL YOUTH AND CREATED...
...THE HOMUNCU-LUS, A SMALL LIVING BEING IN THE FORM OF A HUMAN!
I KNOW ALL THAT, FRANKENSTEIN!
SO YOU CONTINUE AND CONTINUE TO PERSIST! YOU PERSIST IN RIDICULING YOUR PROFESSORS, IN DISCREDITING OUR HON-ORABLE INSTITUTION?!!
WELL THEN! SO, I HEREAFTER FORBID YOU TO USE COURSE MATERIAL SUCH AS HUMAN REMAINS OUTSIDE OF YOUR COURSES!
UNTIL NOW, I'D MADE NO ASSUMPTIONS ABOUT YOUR CHARACTER, YOUNG MAN.
YES, I WAS HESITATING...I WAS HESITATING BETWEEN A YAHOO AND AN ENLIGHTENED SCIENTIST...NOW I KNOW.

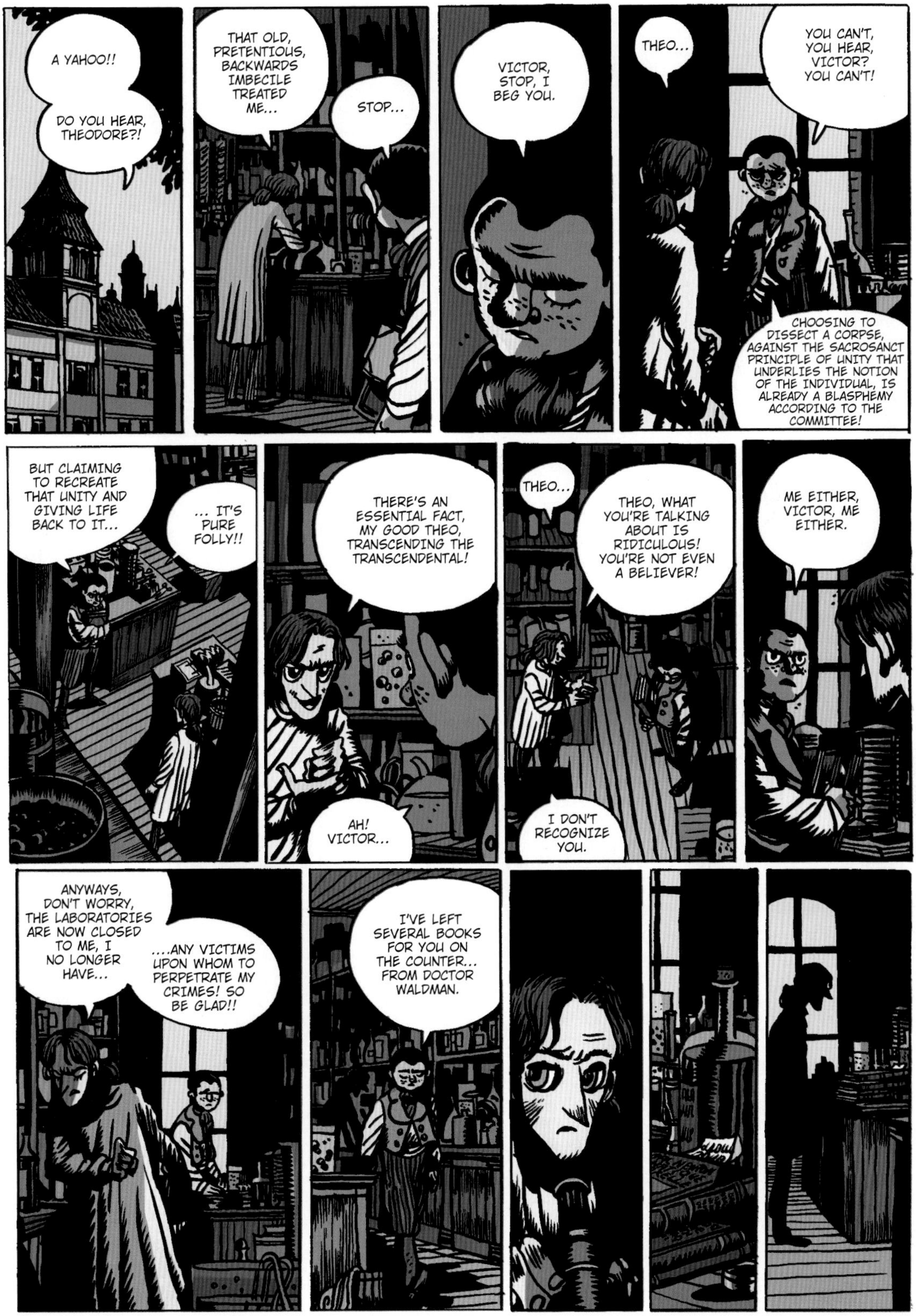
A YAHOO!!
DO YOU HEAR, THEODORE?!
THAT OLD, PRETENTIOUS, BACKWARDS IMBECILE TREATED ME...
STOP...
VICTOR, STOP, I BEG YOU.
THEO...
YOU CAN'T, YOU HEAR, VICTOR? YOU CAN'T!
CHOOSING TO DISSECT A CORPSE, AGAINST THE SACROSANCT PRINCIPLE OF UNITY THAT UNDERLIES THE NOTION OF THE INDIVIDUAL, IS ALREADY A BLASPHEMY ACCORDING TO THE COMMITTEE!
BUT CLAIMING TO RECREATE THAT UNITY AND GIVING LIFE BACK TO IT...
... IT'S PURE FOLLY!!
THERE'S AN ESSENTIAL FACT, MY GOOD THEO, TRANSCENDING THE TRANSCENDENTAL!
AH! VICTOR...
THEO...
THEO, WHAT YOU'RE TALKING ABOUT IS RIDICULOUS! YOU'RE NOT EVEN A BELIEVER!
I DON'T RECOGNIZE YOU.
ME EITHER, VICTOR, ME EITHER.
ANYWAYS, DON'T WORRY, THE LABORATORIES ARE NOW CLOSED TO ME, I NO LONGER HAVE...
....ANY VICTIMS UPON WHOM TO PERPETRATE MY CRIMES! SO BE GLAD!!
I'VE LEFT SEVERAL BOOKS FOR YOU ON THE COUNTER... FROM DOCTOR WALDMAN.

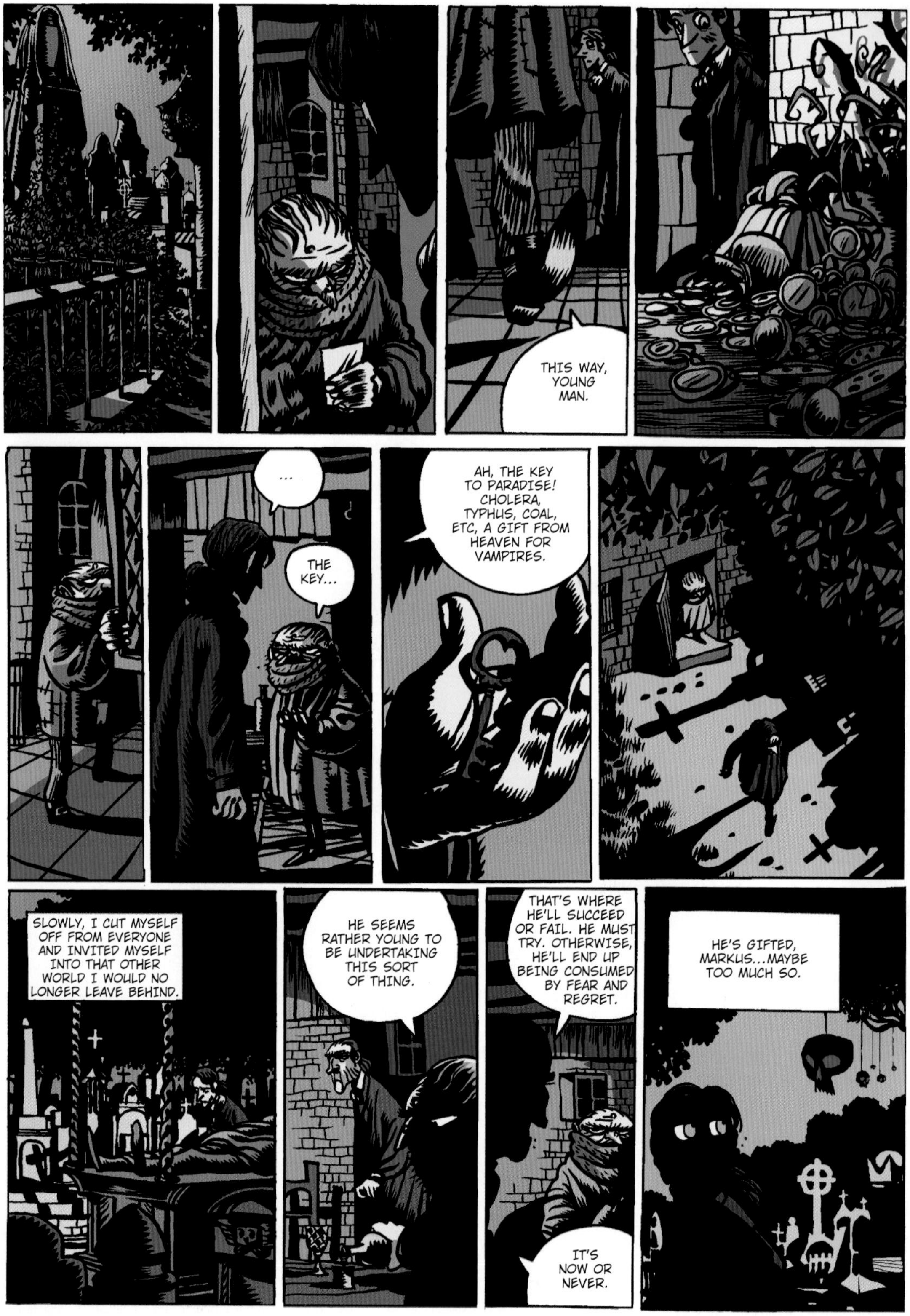
THIS WAY, YOUNG MAN.
...
THE KEY...
AH, THE KEY TO PARADISE! CHOLERA, TYPHUS, COAL, ETC, A GIFT FROM HEAVEN FOR VAMPIRES.
SLOWLY, I CUT MYSELF OFF FROM EVERYONE AND INVITED MYSELF INTO THAT OTHER WORLD I WOULD NO LONGER LEAVE BEHIND.
HE SEEMS RATHER YOUNG TO BE UNDERTAKING THIS SORT OF THING.
THAT'S WHERE HE'LL SUCCEED OR FAIL. HE MUST TRY. OTHERWISE, HE'LL END UP BEING CONSUMED BY FEAR AND REGRET.
IT'S NOW OR NEVER.
HE'S GIFTED, MARKUS...MAYBE TOO MUCH SO.

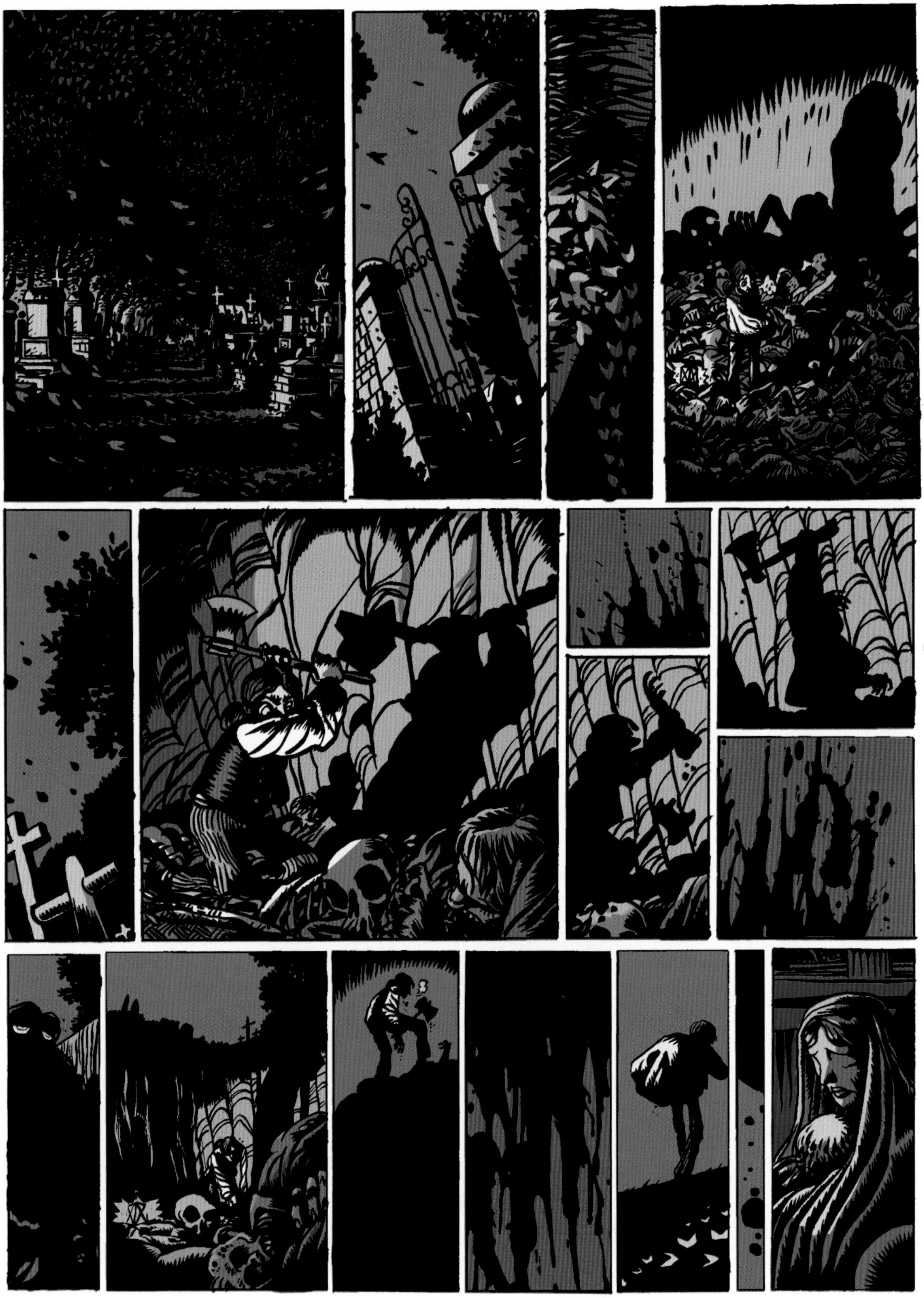

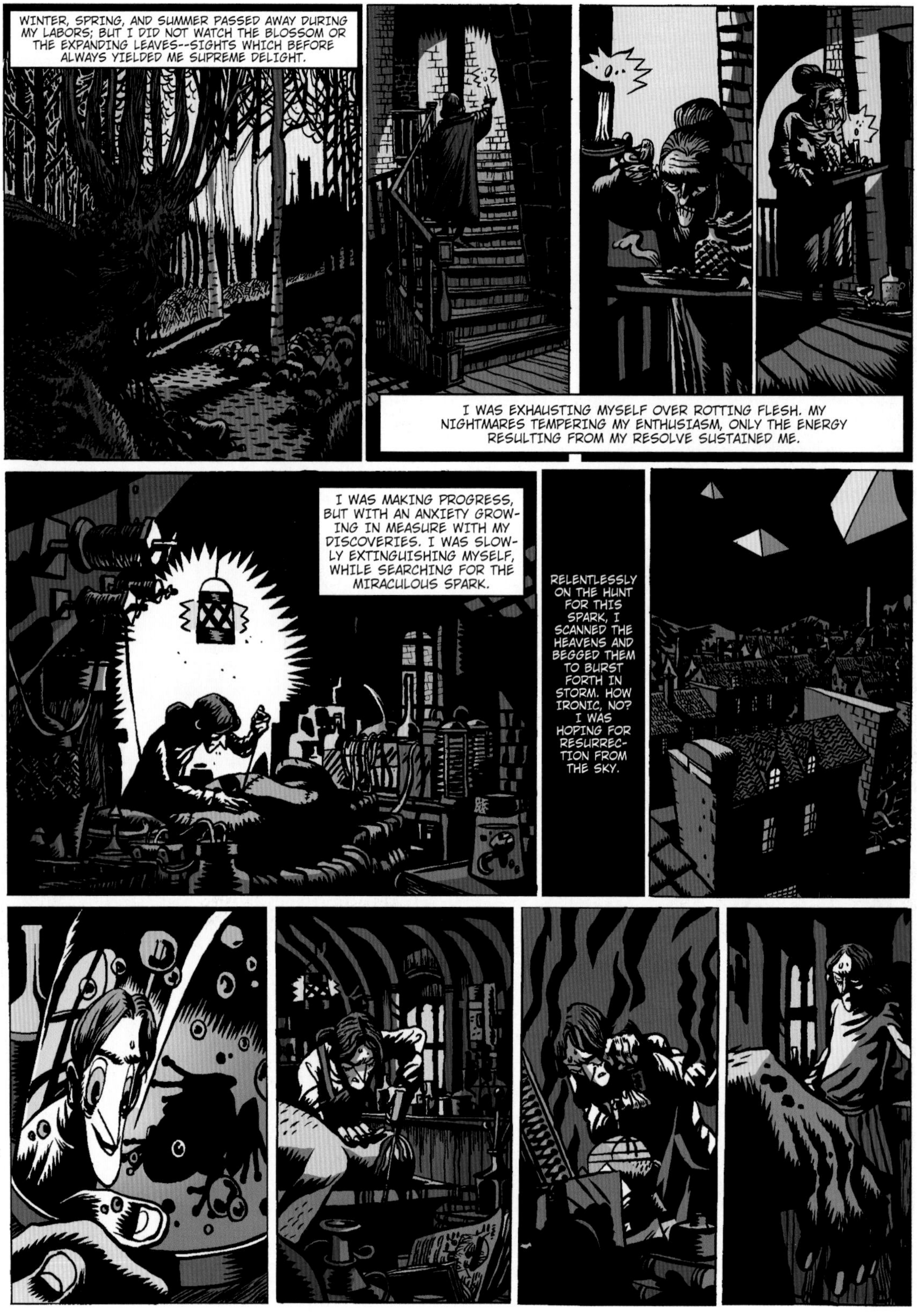
WINTER, SPRING, AND SUMMER PASSED AWAY DURING MY LABORS; BUT I DID NOT WATCH THE BLOSSOM OR THE EXPANDING LEAVES--SIGHTS WHICH BEFORE ALWAYS YIELDED ME SUPREME DELIGHT.
I WAS EXHAUSTING MYSELF OVER ROTTING FLESH. MY NIGHTMARES TEMPERING MY ENTHUSIASM, ONLY THE ENERGY RESULTING FROM MY RESOLVE SUSTAINED ME.
I WAS MAKING PROGRESS, BUT WITH AN ANXIETY GROWING IN MEASURE WITH MY DISCOVERIES. I WAS SLOWLY EXTINGUISHING MYSELF, WHILE SEARCHING FOR THE MIRACULOUS SPARK.
RELENTLESSLY ON THE HUNT FOR THIS SPARK, I SCANNED THE HEAVENS AND BEGGED THEM TO BURST FORTH IN STORM. HOW IRONIC, NO? I WAS HOPING FOR RESURRECTION FROM THE SKY.

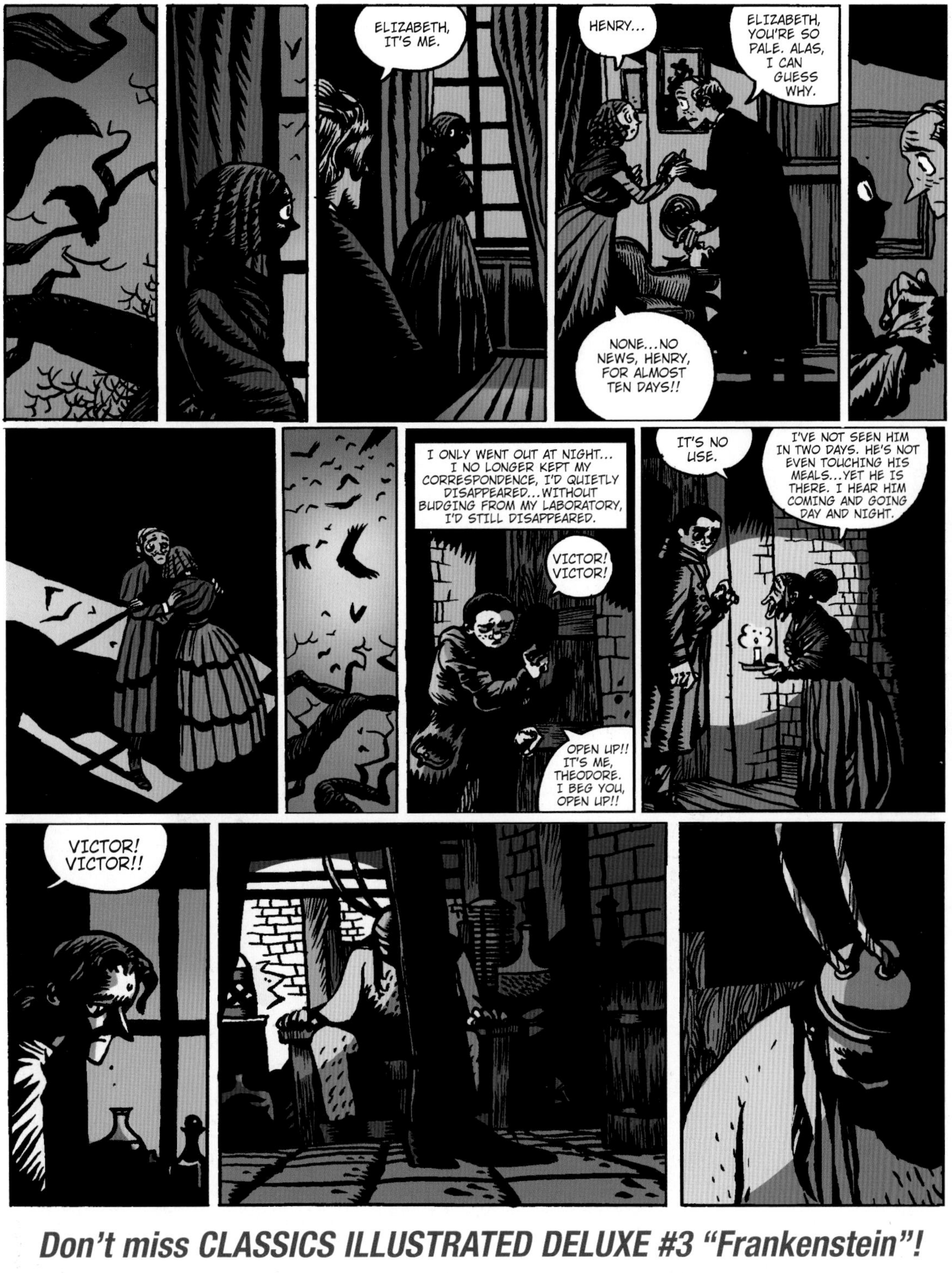
ELIZABETH, IT'S ME.
HENRY...
ELIZABETH, YOU'RE SO PALE. ALAS, I CAN GUESS WHY.
NONE...NO NEWS, HENRY, FOR ALMOST TEN DAYS!!
I ONLY WENT OUT AT NIGHT... I NO LONGER KEPT MY CORRESPONDENCE, I'D QUIETLY DISAPPEARED...WITHOUT BUDGING FROM MY LABORATORY, I'D STILL DISAPPEARED.
VICTOR! VICTOR!
OPEN UP!! IT'S ME, THEODORE. I BEG YOU, OPEN UP!!
IT'S NO USE.
I'VE NOT SEEN HIM IN TWO DAYS. HE'S NOT EVEN TOUCHING HIS MEALS...YET HE IS THERE. I HEAR HIM COMING AND GOING DAY AND NIGHT.
VICTOR! VICTOR!!

Don't miss CLASSICS ILLUSTRATED DELUXE #3 "Frankenstein"!

GAHAN WILSON

Gahan Wilson, whose work appears regularly in *The New Yorker* and *Playboy*, is among the country's best-known and most popular cartoonists. Wilson's macabre cartoons and illustrated stories also have appeared in numerous collections and anthologies, and in publications as diverse as *Omni, Fantasy & Science Fiction, National Lampoon, Weird Tales, Gourmet, Punch* and *Paris Match* magazines. He also has written and illustrated several children's books, including a series on Harry, the Fat Bear Spy, and has written two mystery books: *Eddy Deco's Last Caper* and *Everybody's Favorite Duck*. In his own words: "Gahan Wilson is descended from such authentic American folk heroes as circus and freak king P.T. Barnum and silver-tongued orator William Jennings Bryan. He was officially declared born dead by the attending physician in Evanston, Illinois. Rescued by another medico who dipped him alternately in bowls of hot and cold water, he survived to become the first student at the School of the Art Institute of Chicago to admit he was going there to learn how to become a cartoonist."

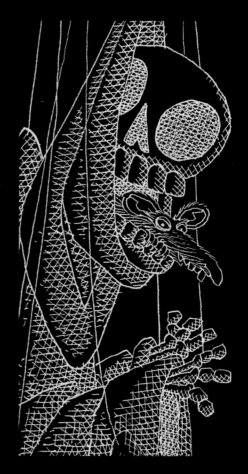